About the Author

Leslie Williams is a US Army veteran and Cameron University
graduate who lives in Oklahoma with her three children and two
cats.

We Did Something About It

Leslie Williams

We Did Something About It

Olympia Publishers
London

www.olympiapublishers.com
OLYMPIA PAPERBACK EDITION

A CIP catalogue record for this title is
available from the British Library.

ISBN: 978-1-80074-070-9

This is a work of fiction.
Names, characters, places and incidents originate from the writer's
imagination. Any resemblance to actual persons, living or dead, is
purely coincidental.

First Published in 2021

Olympia Publishers
Tallis House
2 Tallis Street
London
EC4Y 0AB

Printed in Great Britain

Dedication

For Amanda Johnson

Acknowledgements

I would like to thank Olympia Publishing for taking a chance on this novel, and on me. Thank you to my family for all the support and encouragement: Darrel and Julie Williams, Darrel and Amanda Williams, Jessica Hobert, my children, and Daniel. Operation Underground Railroad is a legitimate organization that actually rescues children and works with law enforcement to stop sex trafficking. You can find more about them at ourrescue.org. Also, if you recognize the signs of human trafficking the National Human Trafficking Hotline is 1 (888) 373-7888.

I would like to tell you how I became a serial killer.

Yes, I Emelia Burke, of Pratt, KS, President of the Student Council, valedictorian of Kansas State University, mother of two, and one of the most boring people in existence, am a serial killer.

First, let me tell you what my life was like. I woke up around five a.m., ran six to seven miles (ten on a bad day), showered, drank coffee and ate my wholewheat toast while I read the paper. I helped the kids get ready for school, though they rarely need much help being fairly independent and reliable, I usually just fussed over them a little until they brushed me off with a hug and a quick "Love you" before heading out to school. Then I went to work, researching, writing, squeezing in counseling sessions with troubled children when I could. Picked up the kids, jujitsu three nights a week for all of us, a quick dinner together, then they did their homework or whatever teenagers do when they pretend to do homework. They usually came and sat on the couch next to me while I read and told me a little about their day before heading to bed. I liked that part. Then I would spend a couple of hours researching and go to bed myself, making room for our cat, Max, at the foot of the bed on the corner of my fluffy comforter. On the weekends, the kids would go with their dad I usually spent extra time at the gym and researching and almost always went on a long, exhausting run. Running is my escape, though it never really occurred to me what I was escaping from.

I liked our busy lifestyle and couldn't imagine anything different. I enjoyed routine, knowing what comes next, predictability. Perhaps it was my traditional Midwest upbringing, or my time in the military, but there is something deeply satisfying about being surrounded by order and structure. Perhaps that's the key to how this all began. Chaos and disorder had no place in my life and if I could change that I usually did.

This was usually an easy fix for someone with my lifestyle, until an idea gets in your head. It's a constant, itching, living idea that becomes so overwhelming it becomes rational. And this rational/irrational thing lives there until it becomes so real that not doing it isn't an option anymore.

But it wasn't entirely my fault.

1
2012

I stood backstage trying to remind myself not to tuck my hair behind my ear, which apparently is my nervous tic. I had gone to the hair salon for this momentous event to have my hair and makeup done, since I rarely give much thought to my appearance. The stylist chatted me up, the way stylists always do, and made me feel more comfortable about changing my look. She turned me around in the chair and my jaw dropped. She had made my long, brown, mousy hair somehow wavy and voluminous and it framed my face in a way I could never reproduce, no matter how many times I tried. The stylist giggled as I leaned in to see that not only had she made me look five years younger with her incredible makeup skills, but she made my dark blue eyes sparkle, even though people rarely noticed or commented on them. Needless to say, she earned that tip.

As I paced backstage in my nicest suit practicing my introduction, and reminding myself of the numbers in the data I would be presenting, it took all my focus to keep my hands off my hair. Public speaking wasn't the issue, I had been teaching all through graduate school and felt perfectly comfortable teaching bored undergrads about the joys of psychology. But this day the audience was filled with scholars, researchers, and statisticians prepared to critique my dissertation, which had already been selected for publication by a prestigious academic journal. This was unheard of in the scientific community, so I was fully expecting an onslaught of criticism from "experienced" academicians who felt my publication was too hasty.

"And now, I would like to introduce Dr. Emelia Burke of Dartmouth and her presentation on Revising the Criteria for Sex Trafficking Reporting. Dr. Burke?"

I took a deep breath and strode across the stage to the podium. The presentation went as expected, I discussed the case studies I had done with victims, explaining the long conversations about how they were treated in public and what could make them more easily identifiable. I showed the graphs of the data I extrapolated from those studies and explained my proposition for changing the reporting criteria for mandated reporters and disseminating this information to the general public. When I talked about my research, I lost all nervousness and fell naturally into my teaching demeanor. This particular topic is naturally very emotionally charged, so I had to keep it as data based and objective as possible to appeal to the scientific community and give my research the credibility it deserved. I completed the presentation with a map showing just how big the sex trafficking problem is worldwide and was met with a round of enthusiastic applause. I fielded the standard questions about data collection and statistical analysis, further research opportunities, methods I used. I tried to humbly defer any compliments to the team of researchers who assisted, but honestly this was one of my proudest moments. I had dedicated years of my life to this research and felt damn proud of the end result. The last question was from a tall young man with a mop of dark curly hair, likely an undergrad, who surprised me by asking, "How did you get into the field of sex trafficking in the first place? Is there a personal connection to this particular topic?" He smirked a little as he sat back down.

"Umm..." I stammered. He cornered me into a personal

question that I didn't expect from an audience such as this, and it threw off my aura of calmness momentarily. "I was fortunate enough to enter my internship right after a big trafficking ring was discovered and there were too many victims for the local mental health community to take on. So, I was allowed the privilege of helping these women and children cope with the trauma they endured. Through the stories they told me I began to identify certain similarities in situations that led them to be victimized and decided the best way to address this is to change the criteria for reportable observations."

The young man stood up again and asked me with a straight face, "Do you think it will change anything?"

Excuse me? Of course it will you moron! was my first thought, so I hesitated. I responded, "Hopefully." He smiled, gave me a quick nod, then sat down.

This led to an awkward pause in the event while the moderator slowly ambled to the mic. My word, "Hopefully" seemed to linger over my entire presentation making me feel more like a naïve activist than a credentialed researcher. I smiled nervously at the audience and walked offstage, flustered by the unexpected question. I walked straight to the refreshment table in the lobby and picked up a small glass of wine to cool my nerves. Other presentations were wrapping up so the lobby was filled with people milling about discussing the exciting possibilities of all the new research they were hearing about. Research conferences can seem dull to a layman, but to a scientist it's like Christmas. I felt anything but jovial as I tried to avoid any of the larger groups so I could collect myself.

"I enjoyed your presentation," I heard behind me. I turned to see the curly haired man smiling at me with mischievous brown eyes.

"Thank you," I replied curtly. I looked around the room.

"Seriously," he continued, with a Middle Eastern accent, "the research is fantastic. I'm only wondering if you chose this because..." he looked me up and down, "perhaps you were a victim?"

"My interest is academic," I met his eyes and he nodded.

"Hmm... perhaps we could discuss this further over drinks in my room later? I am presenting in half an hour on a similar topic and would love to collaborate." He smiled again as I gaped at his casual, wrinkled, button up shirt and jeans.

"You're presenting? I thought you were an undergrad? Just how old are you?" I blurted out.

He laughed good-naturedly, "I'm older than I look. And yes, I'm presenting. But about my proposition?" He clearly was used to women responding quickly to such propositions, being a young, handsome, academic. "I mean, for collaboration," he smiled.

"I will see your presentation, but no to the drinks. I'm a married woman and my interest in *you* is academic as well," I said, hoping to match his confidence.

He laughed again as he walked away, "Your husband is a lucky man!" he called over his shoulder, a little too loudly. I tucked my hair behind my ear and sipped my wine, considering skipping his presentation altogether. I looked through the conference program, realizing I didn't even know when it was, where it would be, or who he even was, and I saw "Sex trafficking Algorithms and Predictions" in the computer science division by a graduate student named Ravi Weiss. I had to admit to myself, I was very curious about what that meant, and I found myself seated in a room full of computer science gurus, looking very out of place.

As Ravi approached the mic, he noticed me and smiled again and began speaking. I was stunned. This young grad student had created a program that could identify trafficking hotspots based on related sociological factors and could even predict where the next hotspot would likely occur. He did some real-world testing with the FBI, for which they were profoundly grateful, and together they were able to rescue a dozen victims and arrest four criminals. THIS was why he was so confident and so interested in my research, the two go hand in hand. He concluded his presentation humbly thanking his team and the FBI for the opportunity to make a difference in the world. The room erupted in thunderous applause. The kid was a prodigy, without a doubt, and everyone wanted in on what he was working on. Someone asked, "How will you disseminate this program to law enforcement? And how can you be certain they will use it?"

"I don't need to; I've already sold the software and the rights to the FBI."

A gasp arose from the crowd. Not only had he created it and tested it, but he probably brokered a huge deal with the FBI all on his own.

"What is your next project? Have you assembled a team? Who will you be working for when you graduate? How many offers are you currently fielding?"

"I guess you'll have to wait to see my name in the headlines," he remarked with a mischievous grin.

The conference was ending, and everyone was lingering too long over the drinks and having intense discussions, as academicians tend to do. My team and I had spent the requisite amount of time discussing our research with other professionals, but I was exhausted and ready to go home. I reached for my coat and Ravi grabbed it, deftly helping me into it.

"Are you sure you won't reconsider drinks?" he leaned close to my ear. I felt warmth rising in my cheeks as I felt a little, not unpleasant shiver.

"I need to get home to my children." I buttoned my coat and stepped away. I regarded him for a moment, the prodigy. "Here is my card, if you really want to collaborate sometime." I hurried to the parking lot through the chilly evening, wishing I had his technical capabilities but reluctant to commit to working with him. I didn't expect to hear from Ravi Weiss any time soon.

2014
London

Speaking engagements had become second nature to me. I spent the last two years working with government officials on how to turn my proposal (now a book) into the Gold Standard on identifying trafficking victims and gave presentations to schools, state health departments, medical conferences, and numerous non-profits. This last stop was by far the most exciting because it was in London, which means "We're going global!" as my agent so enthusiastically put it. Today I would be speaking to The Human Trafficking Foundation, a group designed to integrate and organize efforts of non-government organizations devoted to the cause. They were big on the latest information regarding intervention, so my work caught their attention. In order to attract high value donors, they make it a glitzy affair, though that seemed a little ironic to me still, spending money to get money.

I had also traded in my concern for how "serious intellectuals" should look in favor of how I liked to look. I cut my hair into a swingy bob, traded my Prada sunglasses for sleek Prada reading glasses and tended to wear more dresses than severe and serious looking suits. At this point in my career, my credentials spoke for themselves and I wasn't overly concerned about what anyone else thought of my appearance. I opted for my favorite navy wrap dress and simple heels for this event, foregoing the nightmare of shopping for a gown.

I spoke to the crowd of donors and supporters for a polite twenty minutes, breaking down my initiative into a quick overview of how we're changing the system in the United States. I ended with the required plea to support this cause and the work we are all doing, to which the crowd clapped appropriately, though I questioned how many of them actually really caught the gist of what I was saying while ordering more drinks and patting each other on the back for committing to such an important cause.

I had just sat down at an empty table and slipped my heels off when a glass of champagne appeared in front of me. Ravi Weiss, in a designer suit sat next to me casually as if we had known each other for years. He grinned at me from under that curly, dark, hair, "Lovely speech, inspired me to give half a year's salary." He laughed at himself, probably because he knew that a half year's salary for him could fund this group for years. I sighed.

"The prodigy grew up," I said, amused. "Still working with the FBI?"

"Oh no, I finished MIT and started work with the Israeli government." At this he lowered his voice, "Top secret stuff, very James Bond," he said with a wink.

"Ah, so you are one of the big donors invited then. I should feel honored to be speaking with someone of your stature." I wasn't trying to insult him, but sarcasm slips out naturally sometimes when I'm stressed.

"Oh, the honor is all mine," he grinned. "Actually, I was hoping to discuss the possibility of collaborating. You once gave me your card and made the offer, I'll never forget."

I considered this. Was he being condescending? Was he trying to pick me up?

"What did you have in mind? Are you working on a project now? Has the FBI software taken off?" Now I was curious.

"This really isn't the place to be discussing it. Could we go somewhere a little more private? There is a great pub down the street, you can get the true British experience," he offered.

I hesitated. I didn't want to give him the wrong idea, but my curiosity about his work was burning. "Ok, let's go."

As we walked the short distance to the pub, I noticed he had definitely improved his fashion sense but still had that cockiness about him that I found so off-putting at the conference. There was, however, beneath it a slight sound of defeat. This seemed so out of place in a successful government hacker, so I listened a little closer as he spoke on and on about the more trivial aspects of his current life. He had a beautiful flat in Jerusalem, spent lots of time with the ladies, was an active player in the nightclub scene, and had considered investing in a club but changed his mind. At this last statement something dark flashed in his eyes. I pondered this and decided to find out more about it later.

The pub was, indeed, the quintessential British experience. It was small, cozy, had a fire blazing in the fireplace, and didn't seem very busy. Ravi led me to a table near the fireplace in a somewhat secluded nook. The entire place had an oaky smell to it and a general woodsy feel. He gestured to the bartender to bring two beers and the trivial, light conversation ended abruptly.

"I need you to be completely honest with me, Emelia. Has your initiative worked? Have you seen an increase in the number of arrests or rescues?"

"Excuse me?" This was not the direction I expected this conversation to take.

"Has it?" He said more forcefully.

"Well… we only just really got started. These things take time, I expect to see the numbers go up over time…" I crossed my arms and looked him straight in the eye.

"Time. Of course. That's the same story I got from the FBI," he muttered. Our drinks arrived and he took a sip.

"What do you mean? Your FBI software has instant capabilities, haven't they been using it for what it was intended?"

"That was the idea. But the sex trafficking division can't keep up with it because the bureaucratic process slows it down. By the time they locate a cell, obtain warrants, organize a team, the cell has fallen apart or moved. Same thing is happening in Israel." He looked around suspiciously and lowered his voice. "Israel has bigger fish to fry than pedophile rings that usually pander to the lower class anyway. It's all terrorism, counter-terrorism, spying, political games, really. That's not the job I took but it's the job I do and meanwhile, trafficking happens right under our damn noses." He slammed his fist on the table, spilling a little of his beer and startling the bartender. He gave an apologetic gesture and asked him for a glass of whiskey on the rocks.

"What do you mean lower class? Rich people engage in this, too. Political and economic elite!" I stammered.

"No, no, no, you misunderstand me. It's not the perpetrators who are low class, though some of them are. It's the women and children. Usually minorities, usually poor, usually not missed by the public. It certainly doesn't make international headlines when a homeless girl in India goes missing." His fists were clenched around his glass as he leaned on his elbows and hung his head down.

I considered the truth of his statements. Hadn't I just published about the alarming statistics involving the risk factors for poor and minorities? Had I not seen the reality of how this would play out in the public sphere globally? Is this the key that I had been missing through all my research? I suddenly felt as defeated as Ravi looked, feeling naïve and ineffectual. I took a long drink.

"Ravi, why are you so passionate about this? You asked me how I became involved and I would like to know the same," I asked boldly.

Ravi sighed and finished his whiskey. He looked at his hands for several moments and I wondered if I had crossed some professional boundary. I was about to apologize when he began, "You know I spent four years in the Israeli Defense Forces, right?"

I was stunned. "You are a veteran?"

"Of course, I'm Israeli. I trained with a group that investigated bombings. We looked at debris and analyzed it to determine if the explosive was homemade or commercial, how big it was, and other more technical aspects involving all my spectacular computer skills," he grinned a little at this. "My team became very close over time, in fact, we still spend time together when we can. My partner was Hassan, he is my complete opposite, but we work well together. He understands me like no one else," he gestured with his glass at this, spilling a little. I realized Ravi may be a little drunk, but I was too intrigued to stop his story.

"Hassan and I were sent to analyze the debris in a restaurant that had been bombed by a suicide bomber. We needed to get samples for analysis to try to confirm our suspected identity and affiliation of the bomber. The front of the building had been completely destroyed, the second floor collapsed and there were many, many bodies." He took a deep breath. "We had to approach from the rear of the building, and when we got to the back, we opened the door to find an entirely different looking building. There were rooms on both sides of a long hallway, like a hotel, only seedier. When we looked inside, we found dozens of women and children. Many had been injured in the blast but were too afraid to come out when the fire and rescue teams arrived. Emelia, these children were in rags and expected us to... no, it's too gruesome to discuss." He shook his head as if to erase that memory.

"Hassan immediately picked up two children and carried them outside, so I followed his lead. He always was a better leader. We evacuated as many as we could, many were already dead. We radioed for the police, and this is when I really began to understand how this all works." Ravi leaned forward. "The police didn't identify them or call their families, one officer called the owner of the restaurant and claimed he had some of his 'property' that he needed to come claim." Ravi hung his head for a moment, then leaned back in his seat, crossing his legs. "That's it. That's what made me realize I need to do *something*, even if it doesn't do much good. I'll never forget the looks on their faces when they thought they might finally be free, but then all their hopes were crushed." He shook his head and looked down.

"We have to try, Ravi! I mean, there's only so much we can do. Your software and my initiative will help over time, we just have to give it more time and keep trying!" I realized my fists were clenched, too.

"How much time? And how many lives will be lost in the meantime? Children traumatized? Why doesn't somebody just DO something about it that makes actual changes?" I never knew Ravi had so much passion about this issue, and seeing his emotional reaction to the achingly slow bureaucratic process, the real people he witnessed... I felt his rage in that moment.

I looked at him for several moments. He believed strongly that more should be done, but how much more? And he was IDF, how much did that affect his thoughts on how things should be handled?

"You know, I'm a veteran, too," I whispered.

"You? Seriously?" He leaned closer.

I nodded. "Two combat tours as a medic. I saw a lot of things happen in both Iraq and Afghanistan that weren't exactly 'by the book' but they accomplished the mission. We did what we had to do. Veterans deal with problems in different ways than civilians, but I think you know that. What happened to the officer who called the business owner?" I kept my eyes on his. He hesitated, never losing my gaze, then gave a slow nod. "We did what we had to do," he said quietly.

"Ravi, I need to tell you something between you and I. Something I've never told anyone else…"

2
2013
Miami

"Tomorrow is the big day! Are you super excited?" My office assistant, Gina, bounced into my office and sat on my desk.

"Yes, I am. Got the hotel booked, ready to drink some Mai-Tais and relax in the sun," I replied with a reluctant smile.

"When is Bryce picking up the kids?" she asked.

"Tonight, I might even drive out after work to get some miles out of the way." It was a long trip down the coast from New Hampshire to Miami and I was eager to get on the road and get started.

Gina frowned. "Mia, it's a vacation, not a business trip. Take your time and enjoy yourself." She looked at her hands and tapped her nails on my desk nervously. "I know the divorce must've been hard on you. It's OK to enjoy yourself a little. Maybe even find some hot summer fling," she wiggled her eyebrows when she said this and made me laugh.

"The kids will be fine, you're still young and hot so you won't have any trouble," she said as she sashayed out of my office. "Drink one for me!" she said with a wink before leaving for the day.

I shut down my computer and leaned back in my chair. I envisioned myself running on the beach as the sun rises, all alone with the ocean. A luxurious private cabana with endless fruity drinks, snorkeling, swimming, room service, and sun. Maybe Gina was right about having a fling, too. I laughed as I gathered my things and left the office for my first vacation since I started working.

The trip down the coast was a long one. But the alone time was nice, and I always enjoyed travelling alone. Bryce was very cordial picking up the children and they didn't seem bothered by the idea of spending three weeks away from home. The divorce *had* been hard for me, Bryce admitted he was just tired of supporting my career and wanted to explore life on his own. At least, that's what he told me. In reality he had already met someone, and while nothing had happened between the two of them it seemed he was just ready to move on. The kids fared surprisingly well through the process, they stayed with me in our big two-story suburban home and the only real difference was Dad wasn't there. They saw him every weekend and everyone was satisfied with the arrangement. It looked all neat and tidy on the surface, but I never let the kids see how deeply hurt I was by Bryce's rejection after being married thirteen years.

I finally arrived in Miami and I checked into the Four Seasons and fell into my cushy bed that would be home for the next two weeks and immediately slept for almost ten hours. While the hotel was nice, Miami in the middle of summer was probably a poor choice for my first solo vacation. My sunrise beach runs were never alone, apparently all the other tourists had the same idea I did so I spent most of my run dodging people trying to capture the perfect sunrise photo or staking their spot on the beach early, which was smart because the beach was insanely crowded to the point of discomfort. All my hopes of private cabanas and serene beach reading were dashed when throngs of tourists were simply everywhere. But nonetheless, I was determined to enjoy my vacation.

Some former colleagues of mine were working at the

University of Miami together on a project and we all decided to meet downtown at a fabulous local restaurant called Truluck's for drinks and a taste of the local cuisine. The dinner was spectacular, local, fresh seafood, and we had just a couple drinks but got completely absorbed in conversations about their project and my book. I left the restaurant at closing time feeling warm, happy, and free. My sundress fluttered in the wind as I walked to my car across the street and I started driving back to the hotel.

One hour later, I was completely lost in the worst part of Miami. I had stupidly left my phone back at the hotel, not wanting anything to interrupt our dinner so I had no GPS and no idea where I was or how to get out of there. As I was looking at street signs, trying to find something familiar, I saw a man and a teenaged girl walking the opposite direction. I was driving slowly, and as I passed the girl lifted her head and made intentional and direct eye contact with me. The man grabbed her arm and yanked her closer.

This is it! These are all the signs! The bruising on the legs, the silent cry for help, walking at night, all the signs!

I decided to park the car and follow them. I had made reports as a counselor to family services of suspected abuse, but the girl I just saw with the oversized T-shirt, frayed shorts, and unwashed hair had all the signs of a victim of trafficking and I had to follow to see if I had been right and if she needed help. I kept my distance for a few blocks but made up the distance when they crossed the street toward an abandoned townhouse with broken windows.

"Hey!" I yelled, jogging straight up to the girl and the man. "Can you help me? I need directions to the Four Seasons, I'm a little lost," I smiled at them to gauge their reactions.

The couple picked up speed a little and he shoved her

roughly onto the porch. She stood on the top step with her arms crossed, head hanging down, so her greasy hair covered her face. "Four Seasons, huh? You're in the wrong part of town sweetheart. You should probably get going," he said nervously. I tried to take in all the details about him, mid 30's, maybe 5'11, 225 pounds, sleeveless blue shirt, sandy blond receding hair, prison tattoo on his left forearm. I wanted to give the police all the details, just in case.

"Is that your daughter?" I decided to get straight to the point.

He looked at her then looked at me again, scratching at his face a little. "Yeah, she's my daughter." I looked at the girl and saw a subtle head shake.

"Do you live here?" I asked.

"Why you askin'?" He was getting defensive.

"Because I don't think she's your daughter and I don't think you live here," I said bluntly.

"You a cop?" he demanded.

"No," I said.

"Then fuck you and your questions," he turned to walk up to the girl, but I had grabbed her quickly and wrapped my left arm around her pulling her away from the house. The move had shocked all of us, so we stood there saying nothing for a moment.

"You ain't takin' her," he said to me suddenly shifting his stance to one of intimidation. It was clear that this man was used to intimidating women, and for some reason this infuriated me. I felt the hot anger rising in my cheeks as we started taking slow backward steps toward the street. I scanned the street to see if anyone was around. Not a soul in sight.

I asked the girl loud enough for him to hear me, "Do you want to come with me? Do you need help?" She hesitated, looking at him then looking at me. She nodded her head. "There, now the lady has made the decision for herself. I'm not *taking* her; she's choosing to come with me." We were still about three blocks from the relative safety of the car, so we would need to be quick. Still watching him, we stepped onto the sidewalk and started moving quicker toward the car.

I could see the man tightening his jaw as he started walking toward us. He reached into his pocket, pulling out a switchblade. In one swift motion, I wrapped my arm around the girl's head to cover her eyes and pulled out my pistol, shooting him once in the head and twice in the chest as he fell to the ground. The girl screamed and her knees buckled, so I helped her to her feet and we ran to the car.

She was still screaming as we climbed in and I started driving, trying to put as much distance between us and the crime scene. Her screams eventually settled into sobs and I began to talk to her, trying to calm her down. "What's your name?"

"Lindsey Fowler," she answered between sobs. She wiped her nose on the sleeve of her T-shirt and I noticed she wasn't wearing a bra or shoes.

"Where are you from, Lindsey?"

"Memphis, Tennessee," that explained the deep Southern drawl.

"Wow, you're a long way from home. How did you end up here?" I asked as gently as I could. My heart was still racing, and my hands were shaking but I didn't want her to see that.

She told me the story of how she met a man online and her mother wouldn't let her see him because he was older, and she was only fourteen. They fought about it repeatedly, and she was sure he was a good guy. She thought she was in love and decided to run away to be with him. It didn't turn out like she hoped. She met up with him and he immediately brought her to Miami against her will, treating her more like an animal than a human.

"I loved him, and I thought he loved me, too. But momma said it ain't safe. She was right," she started crying harder.

"I'm sure your mom misses you a lot," I told her, which made her cry harder.

We had passed a police station, finally, so I drove about six more blocks and parked the car.

"Do you want to go home, Lindsey?"

She nodded, crying softly.

"Here's what I need you to do. You walk into that police station, tell them you hadn't seen..."

"Jeremy," she offers.

"Jeremy, ok, tell them you hadn't seen Jeremy for a couple hours and you were at the place you stay with him. Tell them you got sick of all this and want to go home. Tell them *everything* he did to you. But you can't tell them anything about me or what happened at that house." I was taking a huge chance here.

"Can I ask you sumthin'?" she asked.

"Yes."

"Why'd you kill him?"

I thought about that for a minute. "I'm trained to see when women are being hurt, and I knew he was hurting you. And I know that usually, women in that situation, end up dead and I... I didn't want that to happen to you."

She stopped crying altogether. "Yeah, one day it woulda happened. He beat me a lot, he let those other men beat me, too. I was waiting for the day that he beat me to death, then at least all this would end." It broke my heart hearing such a cynical thought coming from such a young girl.

"So, don't forget, I was never here. I saved your life, now you can save mine." I hoped that would be enough.

31

"Yes. Yes. I can do that." She said with new tears. She wiped her face and finally lifted her head up to prepare to go in. And with that, she was gone.

I watched until she made it inside then drove around Miami until I finally found my hotel, two hours later. I was exhausted and strangely exhilarated, so I washed my hands thoroughly before taking a long, hot shower. Afterwards I snuggled up under my cushy comforter and slept more soundly than I had in years.

I woke up late the next morning, still naked. I slipped on the complimentary slippers, made a cup of coffee, and sipped the gourmet coffee while watching the ocean from my window.

This was the kind of peace I was hoping to find on this vacation.

A week later I was back home in New Hampshire spending the rest of my vacation in the safety of my home. The routine felt nice, and Max enjoyed the extra cuddles during the day. One morning as I was sitting on the deck drinking coffee and decided to look up Florida headlines, just in case. Rookie mistake, I know, but my curiosity got the best of me. My heart tightened a bit when I came upon a headline stating, "Man executed in likely drug related homicide". Drug related. Executed. The rest of the article reassured me that Lindsey kept her word because the police certainly weren't looking for a female psychology professor on vacation. I put my phone down. I stretched luxuriously, feeling my muscles relax from my morning run. I smiled to myself and walked back inside to make breakfast.

2014

London

Ravi and I had leaned in closer during my story, because this was not the type of tale we would want overheard. I tucked my hair behind my ear and waited for his reaction. He folded his hands neatly on the table and took a deep breath.

"Do you realize how dangerous it was to follow a criminal like that? You know you could've been killed?" He stared straight at me.

"Well, yes, I suppose I had been lulled into a false sense of security since I always carry my pistol. In retrospect, yes it was stupid, but I don't regret it." I met his gaze directly.

"Are you carrying now?" he asked.

"Yes."

"In that dress?" His eyes drifted over the low neckline of my dress. "You know this is illegal in this country?"

"Yes."

He shook his head slowly with a slight smile. "And you don't feel guilty?"

"Why should I? I saved her life, took the life of someone committed to hurting people, and basically made the world a little better," I said a little defensively.

He waited a moment, thinking it over, then said softly, "I agree." He gently grabbed my left hand running his fingers over my ring finger.

"And now divorced?" He gave me a smoldering gaze.

"Yes." I swallowed hard.

"Available?"

"No." I pulled my hand back into my lap.

"What? Are you dating someone? Remarried?" The smoldering gaze had turned to genuine disappointment.

"Well, honestly," I looked to the fireplace. "I'm just not that attracted to you."

"Seriously? Not at all?"

I thought of that little shiver the first night we met. "No, not at all." I stifled a giggle.

He nodded his head at this, then reached for my glass (which was half full) and swallowed the rest with one gulp. "Then I believe we'll make excellent partners because I'm not the least bit attracted to you." He regarded me seriously as he said this.

I raised an eyebrow and smiled.

His seriousness broke into a laugh that was impossible not to join. We laughed and laughed, drawing attention from the other bar patrons. This is when I began to truly understand who Ravi was.

3
2017
Manchester-Boston Regional Airport
New Hampshire

"Daddy!" The kids had spotted Bryce and Laura before I had, and Jenna went running to him for a hug. She still had that little girl enthusiasm, though at thirteen she was on the brink of becoming a moody teenager. I saw little moments of moodiness and attitude, but I usually attributed this to her fierceness, which I refused to tame out of her.

Bryce scooped her up into a big swinging hug while Laura leaned over the stroller of baby TJ, her long blond hair hiding her face. Ethan walked over to his dad, almost as tall as him, and gave him a high five and a "man hug" with lots of back patting. He looked achingly grown-up in that moment, reminding me of when he had been a clingy toddler holding tight to my legs everywhere I went. I sighed. Then Laura stood and the kids enveloped her in an exuberant double hug which she returned, laughing. I had worried that baby TJ might take some of her love away from my own children, but she had shown them just as much love as ever. Stepmoms like this don't come around every day, so I was grateful.

"So, Grand Canyon?" I asked them.

"Laura has some family in New Mexico, so we're stopping there first then headed to the big hole in the ground," Bryce laughed at this joke and Ethan rolled his eyes good naturedly. "It should be fun, though, first big vacation for the family."

Jenna piped in, "Mom is going on a vacation, too! She has all these friends she travels with and they go on fun adventures so this time she's going rock climbing in the Dominican! That's so cool, right Dad?" She bounced over to me and I wrapped my arm around her.

"Yeah, that is cool. Good for you, Emelia, you need something like this," Bryce said.

I saw a flash of something—maybe jealousy—in Laura's smile for just a moment.

Don't worry, honey, you have nothing to worry about. I've seen how he looks at you.

"That does sound fun! Machu Pichu last year, the Dominican Republic this summer... your life sounds so exciting," Laura said. She genuinely seemed excited for me, sweeping her hair over her shoulder and smiling widely.

"Yeah, it should be fun. I'll take lots of pictures. Now come give me some hugs before you miss your flight, guys," I reached my arms out and Jenna squeezed me tight.

"I love you, Mom, bye!" and she dashed off with her little suitcase. Ethan hugged me close and told me to be careful with a very serious look. I ruffled his hair, and he shook it off with a smile. I watched them walk toward security and Bryce reached over and gently stroked Laura's long smooth hair. As I walked back to the parking garage I tried to remember if he ever stroked my hair like that. But, no, not any time that I could remember. I sighed and smiled to myself as I tried to switch gears to prepare for my "exciting vacation".

2017

Punta Cana, Dominican Republic

We were a well-oiled machine.

I sipped my Diet Coke and waited for Ravi at a remote table

in the airport lounge. He wasn't due to arrive for another half hour, so I browsed through my research preparing to give him a quick briefing before our "travel group" arrived. This was the system, a two-hour meeting at the airport to lay out the specifics for the operation and to share all the information we had gathered in the previous six months. The travel group, of course, was our cover so it genuinely looked like a vacation. We had photos, alibis, everything we needed to appear as though we were simply two tourists from different parts of the world who enjoyed travelling with a group.

As I looked through my files, I thought back to our first operation. We agreed that both the US and Israel were too hot and too close to home, so we needed to expand our reach. Mexico was a disaster. Over planned, underprepared, and overexcited as we were, we pretty much botched the whole operation. There was a nasty firefight with security due to poor communication, half the women we wanted to rescue had no idea who we were, and since we couldn't speak Spanish, we couldn't explain that we wanted to save them. And, in a surprising twist, there was a girl whose pimp kept her hopped up on meth who attacked me with a knife. I grappled with her until I could get a decent chokehold so Ravi could restrain her, but I took a few good slices. Mostly, I remember Ravi watching a YouTube video on how to do proper sutures while sewing up a nasty gash on my ribcage and pouring me glass after glass of tequila while I criticized his technique. We learned the value of a proper anesthetic in the med kit from that experience.

We only convinced twelve women to come with us and made the mistake of trusting the police. We dropped them in a safe place and called in to report a group of sex trafficking victims and watched from a safe distance. The police arrived quickly, and we watched in horror as the women were arrested for prostitution. Back at the hotel we felt defeated and I almost abandoned the idea altogether, had Ravi not sat me down and gone over every detail and every mistake we made so we could improve for our next operation. We argued and bickered over how it should all be done for hours, but eventually we began to nail down a technique that utilized both of our strengths and abilities. The work showed in the next operation, which saved eighty women and children in Bogatá, Columbia, who we handed over to a non-profit organization that housed victims of trafficking. Non-profits and non-government organizations were our safest bet for getting the victims to safety and maintaining our anonymity.

As we did more missions, we had fewer tactical errors in addition to learning exactly what equipment we needed. That's Ravi's specialty, mine is in the research, groundwork and local recon. His other specialty is the necessity of being a man, especially a charismatic and streetwise man who knew how to find the kind of seedy people we need to lead us to the deepest dens of depravity. Also, his suturing technique has greatly improved, the deft hands of a computer engineer were made for such delicate work, so I trust him more and criticize less. It works like clockwork now, and the order and structure of it gives me a great deal of satisfaction in a job well done. I took another drink and checked the time.

Ravi arrived right on time and we engaged in our normal greeting, a quick handshake.

"Emelia."

"Ravi."

This part was all business, since it had to be quick. He showed me the satellite photos and pings from his tracking program for the most likely area for trafficking, and my research confirmed the location. I described the local gang activity, which was extensive in this part of the city, and we discussed the type of transport and which group we would be working with for rescue. We agreed to take a detour after the rescue to the north part of the island, to take out the main operator of the majority of the trafficking in Haiti, a local gangster who liked to stay close enough to Port-Au-Prince to protect his investments but far enough away to have a luxurious hilltop villa.

"He sounds like a real winner," Ravi commented sarcastically.

"Yeah, without taking him out the process will just repeat itself. I've been hitting the range with my sniper rifle for a few months... what do you think?" I asked.

"Brilliant! But our time is up here, let's go be tourists," he said with an eye roll.

I giggled. He reveled in the attention he got from the group, but pretended to dread it. They all adored him with his big laugh and flirty jokes with the women, though he usually found local women to seduce while we were on these trips. The group all laughed it off, "That Ravi is such a cad!" but I had a hard time reconciling *that* Ravi with the one I knew so well; we barely had to say a word to know when we were moving during operations.

We walked to the terminal discussing work, Bryce and the kids and normal life things. He grew quiet as we waited then leaned close and told me, "Emelia, I have some exciting news that I should probably tell you." His eyes were serious.

"Well, ok, what is it?" I asked. I tucked my hair behind my ear and looked toward the terminal.

He pulled out his phone and was looking through it, perhaps to show me something, when we hear, "Ravi! Emelia! Oh, how we've missed you!" It was Mark and Julia Bannon, the middle-aged English couple who had missed our last couple vacations.

Ravi quickly shoved his phone back in his pocket, "Darlings! We've all missed you! Where have you been? Julia, you look ravishing!" He swept her up in a hug, delighting her to no end. I supposed the exciting news would have to wait.

Generally, the first order of business is dinner at the finest restaurant in town to catch up with each other's lives. This time we had Mark and Julia, a lovely Japanese couple, the Saito's, who barely spoke English but seemed to enjoy our company, the Australian woman, Diana Price, who almost always comes with us, and three other couples from the United States we were mostly familiar with. Dinner was delicious and many drinks were had as we discussed work, kids, politics, and listened to a very lengthy story about Julia's knee surgery that kept them from vacationing with us last time. After about an hour Ravi tapped his glass with his fork and proclaimed, "I have an announcement that many of you may find shocking... I am a father!" The group gasped and my shock was genuine as well. *A father?* He never made eye contact with me as he pulled out his phone and showed a picture of a dark-haired toddler with Ravi's big brown eyes and an adorable toothy grin. The group oohed and aahed over the photo, congratulating him and welcoming him to the parenting club. I cleared my throat.

"Who is her mother?"

He finally looked at me intensely. Then jumped right back into character. "Her mother was a Eurotrash girl I dated for a couple months a few years ago. She had the baby and decided not to tell me, but I guess mothering got old, so she brought her to me. Her family has loads of money and they all adore Nera, so they take her during summer and Christmas break to spoil her and give me time to relax and get back to the old Ravi," he smiled mischievously at the group at this, getting a good laugh from those who knew him.

"I propose a toast!" Mark loudly, and drunkenly proclaimed. "To Ravi and baby Nera!"

I raised my glass and took a long drink. The implications of this for our operations were unknown and I hated being caught off guard. I excused myself for the evening and went to my hotel. It had been a long and exhausting day, so I undressed completely and crawled under the covers and fell immediately asleep.

"Mia, Mia, wake up."

Still half asleep, I opened one eye to see Ravi sitting on my bed. "How did you get in here?" I mumbled groggily.

He groaned, "I hacked the lock, of course. Now wake up, Mia, I need to talk to you about this."

He only called me Mia when I was angry, and he was trying to calm me down. I was trying, in my half-asleep state to remember if we had a fight.

"I should've told you earlier, but I knew you would be angry. Nera will not affect my ability to do this operation or any operation. Everything is the same, I promise." He looked serious and determined with his furrowed brow.

"Wait, no, Ravi, I'm not angry. Just surprised. And concerned. Having kids changes people, are you sure you won't worry about leaving Nera an orphan and get distracted? Can you still do this without making a mistake that will get you killed?" I sat up on my elbow, covering myself with the thick blanket.

"No, I'm fully committed." He sounded a little too adamant about it.

"Here, lay down and tell me about her. Tell me all of it," I told him.

He laid down next to me and told me the whole story of the mother who cried to him that raising a child just wasn't something she wanted to do and just left. He told me how terrified he was, holding this one-year-old child with no idea how to even care for a child and how he looked into her beautiful eyes and fell madly in love. So, he had outfitted his entire flat with children's toys and childproofed everything. He discussed the difficulty of finding quality childcare, the simple joys of taking her to the park or shopping and how he loved to dress her in tiny designer clothes with matching bows in her dark curly hair. He didn't complain about the sleepless nights or temper tantrums or having to change his lifestyle, it was only about how full his life was now and how perfect Nera was. It was a Ravi I had never known and never expected, but I smiled when he pulled out her picture again and hugged it to his chest and said, "Mia, she's my light. My little light."

I smiled and said, "Having kids changes everything, doesn't it?"

He laughed heartily, "I never realized! It's a love I've never experienced!"

I thought about what he might have meant by that but dozed off before I could reach a conclusion. I awoke later to find him still there sleeping soundly next to me. I went back to sleep, glad for the comfort of a familiar body next to mine.

4
2017
Port-Au-Prince, Haiti

Once our tourist week in Punta Cana was over, I was grateful to get down to business. Ravi chartered a flight from Punta Cana to Port-Au-Prince and had made prior arrangements with customs to look the other way when certain things came through in our luggage. I suppose money, and being a high-ranking government official, gets you far in some places. Ravi found our house for the next three weeks, booked under a false name with perfectly forged documents to back it up. He really could do just about anything with a computer. It was a sizeable and private cottage at one of the resorts, we would need the space for the planning phase of the operation. Ravi unloaded all our gear, and we did a quick layout of all we would need for each part of this operation. Helmets, Kevlar vests, pistols with suppressors, my sniper rifle equipped with a regular scope and an infrared scope courtesy of the Israeli government. I asked Ravi how he gets away with "borrowing" all this equipment, it seemed a little risky.

He shrugged. "You can get away with almost anything if you do it with confidence. I walk in and request the equipment, they assume I am taking it to the lab for some upgrades, and nothing is ever said about it." He began our regular routine of disassembling the weapons, cleaning all the individual pieces, reassembling, and doing functions checks. I sat down next to him to help and we sat in silence while we went through our normal routine. The tedium of tasks like this is comforting to me; Ravi and I can share silences that aren't awkward.

We fitted the scopes to the rifle, and he picked it up and checked the sights. "Do they look right to you? Is that how you want it?" he asked.

"Looked great when I checked," I shrugged.

"Are you sure this isn't too much firepower for you? I mean, you're 5'5, maybe 130 pounds. This really isn't a lady gun," he said. He glanced at me with his eyebrows raised.

I punched him in the arm hard and he laughed setting the weapon back on the table. "OK, OK, you proved your strength," he walked into the kitchen rubbing his arm playfully while I shook my head and laughed. He started the coffee, and I opened his laptop and logged him in so it would be ready for him. Simple movements like this are like clockwork.

He brought in two cups of coffee and opened the satellite photos so we could get a better look at the "pimp house". Cite Soleil was listed as one of the most dangerous places in the world, and the place we planned to raid was right in the middle. The buildings all looked hastily and poorly constructed and were tightly packed together. His tracking program showed a high amount of business done there and it was at the top of the list for potential victims in the area. "We may have our work cut out for us this time," he said. Our usual approach is two or three days of recon where I "go high" and he "goes low". This means I use video scopes to surveil the target place while he gathers intel and makes connections on the streets to get a foot in the door. Then we take a day to prep a specific approach based on our recon and execute the mission the following morning, which makes it even more difficult to maintain cover, but the vast majority of the business is done at night, making night missions entirely too risky. We learned this the hard way, too.

Taking out the main operator this time changed our normal operation schedule. Usually we raid the house, transport the victims, then head back to our place and clean up and review. The extra steps and deviation from our normal routine had me a little on edge about things. I was tapping a pen against my lip thinking about all the possible contingencies when Ravi threw his T-shirt at me, "Relax, you're no good to me when you stress." He was going into his room to change into appropriate street clothes for his recon; this snapped me out of it and I jumped up to go get ready.

11:30pm

As glamorous as it may sound, doing recon is easily the most boring part of this job. I had found an old church with a high bell tower right outside the unofficial border of Cite Soleil and knew my equipment would still give me enough reach to get good surveillance. Ravi left earlier dressed tourist nice, ready to do business with some of the most evil people on the planet. I wore all black and carried a backpack with my gear. I parked a couple blocks from the church and crept slowly through the alley behind the church, people tend to do their business in places like this and the last thing we needed was an interruption. It seemed clear, no security that I could see.

I hopped the fence, stepping carefully over the barbed wire. The church had a fire escape on the west side of the building that would get me within climbing distance of the roof of the tower. I climbed the steps and pulled myself up on the main roof. The shingles were loose and in a serious state of disrepair, so I would have to tread lightly. I took my time getting to the bell tower and bingo! The tower had a small grate I was able to remove and crawl inside. It was dusty and the stairs creaked, but they took me to the very top with a window facing the city. This luck was

45

almost unbelievable, but I set up my equipment, stacked up a couple of boxes I found in the hallway and was comfortably seated, scanning the city for our target within minutes.

Then, the waiting game. I set up the infrared and night scopes, which both transmitted the video straight to Ravi's laptop when I toggled a switch. I saw a lot of men going in and out of the building, but nothing to really give us anything to work with. Around three, however, business started to slow, so the girls opened up the wide windows behind a dozen or so pieces of rebar and began to catcall the men walking down the street, presumably to attract more customers. I flipped the switch to record this. Since tonight's shift covered until four a.m., I packed up my things but left the boxes in place for tomorrow night and slipped out the same way I came in. By the time I reached the cottage, Ravi had already finished and was asleep in his room. Exhausted as I was, I was eager to hear how his night went and what he found out. But that's not the routine so I went to my room and quickly fell asleep.

Late the next morning, I padded to the kitchen sleepily, wearing only a long T-shirt and panties, standard sleeping attire in this heat. Ravi was cooking something and turned around to hand me a cup of coffee, two sugars, plenty of cream.

"Love the hairdo, you should keep it like that," he said with an impish grin.

I smiled and ruffled it more to make him laugh and turned on his laptop while he finished breakfast. I stood at the window and watched the ocean while sipping coffee. It seemed watching the ocean was the only time my brain switched off. Just wave after wave, never ending. I heard Ravi bringing breakfast to the table, so I went into the kitchen to make his coffee, dark with one sugar. We sat down and had breakfast while reviewing the recon

I did.

"Yes," he said through a mouthful of bagel, "the people I spoke to told me this was the place I needed to go. It's controlled by one of the bigger gangs in Soleil so they're likely to have people watching from everywhere. But I have an idea."

"Ok, what is it?" I asked.

"You'll have to find out later tonight, I need to do some more work on this first. But... I think I can do it. Yes, this I can do." I didn't like the uncertainty in his voice.

"Can you do it or not? We need to know this, Ravi!"

"Mia, Mia, relax. I got this covered," he was always so calm about these things.

We bickered over the details of the evening for the rest of the morning, then decided to head out for lunch. I have a sixth sense for local places with good food and we found a little bistro that served amazing conch fritters with Blan Manje for dessert. Full, relaxed, and happy, we drove back to the cottage to get some rest before starting the night's work. Singing at full volume along with a Sublime song on the ride home made us both laugh and feel as though we really were on vacation for a few moments.

Ravi was gone when I woke up, so I gathered my gear and returned to my recon position. It was largely uneventful, until a truck pulled up to the front of the building. The security there started unloading women and children from the back of the truck roughly, shoving them when necessary. Some of the children were so small they had to be carried. I shook my head, no matter how many times I saw children being treated like this, it never got easier. It always infuriated me. I made sure to record this and returned to the cottage to wait for Ravi and go over the satellite images of the surrounding areas. Ravi stumbled through the door around three am, disheveled and looking drunk.

47

"Emelia, I think we got it!" he proclaimed as he stumbled into the kitchen and grabbed a bottle of water. I brought him a couple of ibuprofen and sat him at the table so we could discuss what we "got".

"Well?" I insisted.

"Ok, ok, I'll tell you. First, I went to the opposite side of Soleil and found a bar, threw some money around and raised a little bit of a scene. But it got the attention of the rival gang."

This didn't sound like good news to me. A rival gang? Causing a scene? How was this helpful to the mission?

"I had a long talk with some mid-level guys and told them I was planning on taking out some of their rivals very soon. For personal reasons. Including the gang's main benefactor. They seemed skeptical, and by skeptical, I mean they took me into the alley and roughed me up a bit," and he laughed. I hardly found this funny at this point.

"But they believed me. So, after some negotiation, they agreed to provide us not only a way into the city but security on the way out. They think this will open up some business opportunities in new territory and we can help them achieve those ends," he finished his bottle of water and put his hands out in a "you're welcome" gesture.

"Ravi. That only covers a small portion of what we need to do! Did you recon the house itself? What about transport? Numbers? We need this information!" It sounded like he really missed the mark this time, which was unlike him.

"Mia, you haven't let me finish. I found our transport, like I always do, and went to the north part of the city to check in with our friends at the house. They took me into the building and made offers, but I told them I would need more for a big party tomorrow night. And I told them I want them young. So, they're bringing more from their other locations!"

This was starting to sound a lot better by the second. "That makes sense now, I saw them unloading a lot of people from a truck last night. Ok, how are we getting them out?"

"The rebar over the window. Remember Bogatá? When we tried to cut the rebar, but it was just screwed into the drywall? Same deal. Weak, but giving the illusion of security. You handle security downstairs, give me the signal, and I use the bus to pull out the rebar and unload all the victims onto the top of the bus then into the bus and we literally drive it right out of town with a security escort. You don't have to tell me, I know, I'm brilliant," he smiled grandly.

"Tomorrow morning?" I asked.

"Nine, sharp," he replied.

"Perfect. We leave at eight. You look like you could use a little sleep, though," I looked him over, drunk, a cut below his right eye, and a bruise coming up on his left cheek. He looked wrecked.

"Sleep, God yes." He stumbled down the hall, taking off his clothes as he went and plopped down on my bed.

I sighed. It wasn't the first time we had slept next to each other and I'm sure it wouldn't be the last. I crawled under the covers next to him and stretched out on my stomach leaving plenty of room between us. He was already sleeping and breathing heavily, so I reached up and gently brushed a dark curl off his forehead. Then I set the alarm and slept.

9am

I dropped Ravi off at a shady looking salvage yard to pick up the bus then headed to the entry to Cite Soleil. My contact was supposed to meet me right outside the police checkpoints so we could have easy access to the city. I waited nervously, looking for a tan Toyota, hoping I wouldn't get hassled by anyone while I waited. I finally saw the car pull up and stop, honking impatiently. I got in his car, a skinny dark-skinned man who said nothing as we cruised past the checkpoints without even slowing down. Clearly, he has some pull here and may be on the level about security for us. He dropped me four blocks from the pimp house and said something in French that I didn't understand so I gave him a quick nod of thanks and started walking. I checked my watch, 8:57. Perfect.

The door to the house had an electronic keypad, so I used the device Ravi gave me to disable it in seconds, but it emitted a loud beep when I opened the door. A quick scan of the room showed a filthy couch in one corner and an even filthier one against the left wall, with one of the six security members on it just waking up. He reached for his gun but in a couple of quick steps I was able to reach him and silently put a bullet in his head. *That's one down. Five to go.*

I had to move quickly, so I quietly rounded the corner into the first bedroom on the left and found number two and three sleeping peacefully in twin beds. I pulled out both pistols and shot them simultaneously, feeling very wild west in that moment. *Two and three, halfway there.* I hurried into the next bedroom and quickly executed a man sleeping next to a woman, who started screaming. This meant I only had seconds to get to numbers five and six. I rounded the corner and fired immediately on number five who was running to see what was wrong, I stepped over his body and into the bedroom of number six, quite proud of the time I was making when I threw the door open to find his bed empty. I scanned the room, but he wasn't there. I took a step back and heard the bathroom door open just before an enormous arm wrapped around my neck in a choke hold. I didn't have time to panic, so I kicked off the doorframe to get him off balance and as he came back, I did a textbook hip throw which left him lying on the ground in front of me. I planted a knee in his chest, ID'd him as number six and put a round in his forehead. I radioed Ravi, "Six down" and instantly heard a thunderous crash from upstairs and screaming.

Running up the stairs, I saw Ravi had already taken out the rebar window, and was loading women and children onto the bus. The top of the stairs led to a long hallway with a dozen or so rooms on each side. I went from one room to the next saying the only phrases I knew in French, *"Viens avec moi, je suis là pour te sauver. Nous vous emmènerons dans un endroit sûr!"*, meaning, "Come with me, I am here to save you, we will take you somewhere safe". Most of the women and children looked terrified but followed our directions and moved towards the window. They seemed trained to follow directions, almost brainwashed. Especially the children. One woman stood firm, a child on her hip of maybe three years old. She jutted her chin toward me and said, "You save us? Take us to another place for hurt? No man touch my child, she safe here. She safe there?" My heart ached for this mother, who had managed to keep her child safe through all this.

"Yes. Safe." I put my hand over my heart as a promise, then remembered something. "See," I said, pulling my locket from inside my shirt to show her a picture of my own children. "Safe." She paused a moment, looking at me skeptically, then followed me out into the hallway and toward the gaping hole that had been the window. She and her child were the last to exit the house and Ravi pulled them directly down and helped them onto the bus, which was substantially overcrowded.

I squeezed in as Ravi closed the door. We started driving

away and I asked him, "How many were you expecting?"

He smiled and said, "Fifty, but this looks closer to a hundred." We both smiled at that. As we pulled onto the main road, three motorcycles flanked us and I drew my weapon thinking the worst. "No!" Ravi yelled, grabbing my arm, "It's our security!" he said with raised eyebrows. I held my weapon at the ready, just in case, but these guys looked like serious players in the gang business. We were ten minutes into the drive, the bus was crowded and hot, filled with the whimpers and cries of scared children when the gunfire began. Cars had appeared behind the motorcycles and they were exchanging gunfire, eliciting screams from all our passengers. I motioned for everyone to get down low, but with the overcrowding of the bus, the people could barely move. Ravi sped up, pushing the bus to the very brink, and getting us to the edge of the city. The gangs peeled off in another direction, continuing the fighting while I was grateful to be past that part of the operation. We approached a police checkpoint, and I wondered how we would get past without our "security" escort. Ravi stopped, opened the window, and coolly passed the officer an envelope. He glanced inside and saw what looked like several hundred-dollar bills and waved us through. I shook my head in disbelief at his quick thinking and he just laughed, like he always does.

We parked, as planned, two blocks from the UN building and jogged a couple blocks north before calling my contact at the UN to tell her the package had arrived. We watched as aid workers emptied the bus, offering hugs to the crying women and offering to carry the children. This part of the job was complete, like clockwork. I looked at Ravi, and he was beaming at the children running through the gates of the UN. We shook hands at our success and shared a granola bar before we walked to the parking garage where we had stashed the motorcycle for the next part of the mission.

We tossed our Kevlar vests into a nearby dumpster and stashed our weapons and gear in the backpack so we could look like regular tourists walking the few blocks to the motorcycle. As I took off my Kevlar, Ravi looked at me with alarm.

"What happened to your neck?"

"Ah, just a little problem with number six. Why? How does it look?" I hadn't thought about it really since we left the house.

"It looks like you got choked out." We started walking down the sunny street. "Let's get back to the room and I can put something on that for you. We have time."

"What? No, we don't, the gang members will be calling the head gangster now, we have to move before he beefs up security and makes this impossible!"

"I cut his communications last night. Plus, the gang members are engaging in an all-out war right now, it was a distraction. All part of the plan, darling. You can say it now," he smiled at me.

"Say what?" I was glad for him buying us time but irritated with his cockiness.

"You can say I was right and planned it perfectly so we could hit the gangster under the cover of darkness," he did a silly little dance as we walked. "You were right, Ravi, you're a genius Ravi," he goaded me, laughing.

My neck was feeling sore and might be in need of some kind of treatment, so I suppose his planning was pretty much on point. Maybe I could even get a little rest.

"Ok, you were right, you happy now?" I gave him a playful shove.

"Yes! The almighty Dr. Emelia Burke admitted I was right! Mark this day in the annals of history!" He raised his hands in

53

victory and I laughed at his enthusiasm. Only Ravi could be so playful and sure of himself in the middle of an operation like this. I think he got a burst of energy from seeing the victims being rescued and knowing they were now in a safe place. Also, there was a festive air about this particular area of Port-Au-Prince, it was hard not to feel some excitement at the exotic smells of plantains being roasted and the brightly colored buildings.

Ravi started the bike and revved the engine a few times while I climbed on behind him. He took off smoothly navigating the heavy Port-Au-Prince traffic and I finally started to relax. The first time I rode with Ravi was in India a couple of years prior and I held him so tightly it almost made us crash. We argued for hours that night over whose fault it was, but I relented and now I feel just as comfortable on the back of a bike with him as I would in a car.

When we reached the cottage, I took off my T-shirt and inspected the damage to my neck. Just some bruising and a few abrasions, but Ravi insisted on treating it with some antibiotic ointment while I told him the story of what happened. "It sounds like you could use a backrub, too. That guy probably outweighed you by a hundred pounds!" he said.

"That's where jujitsu lessons pay off," I smiled.

He insisted on using some Icy Hot on my back to prepare for the next part of the operation, and I was too tired to fight it. I laid down on my bed while he massaged my lower back to try to ease the strain. It felt so soothing I fell asleep before he could even finish. I awoke with a start, afraid I had slept too long, when Ravi came in with a sandwich and some coffee. "You were sleeping so peacefully I didn't want to wake you."

"Um, thanks," I said. I realized I was starving so I grabbed the sandwich while he filled me in on the updated satellite photos of the gangster's villa. It was perched on a hill surrounded by trees and had floor to ceiling windows.

"We may get lucky and see him right away, otherwise we'll be in for a long night of waiting," Ravi said with a frown. "We can't take the main road to his house because it will be crawling with security, but there is a highway roughly two miles from his house where we could stash the car, hike in a little and find a good vantage point. Do you feel up to a hike?" He looked at me with concern.

I rolled my eyes and he just laughed. "So, we leave in half an hour. I have everything prepared, but you may want to put a shirt on," he said with a wink. I threw a pillow at him as he backed out of the room laughing.

10pm

"Ravi, quick, I need you to take a look and tell me I'm not seeing what I think I'm seeing."

He was setting up his laptop next to my sniper's perch made of a pile of rocks and a small patch of dirt and he rushed over to look through the scope.

"Shit, he has a boy with him. Is there anyone else in the house?"

"I only saw a profile of a woman sleeping in an upstairs bedroom but what do we do about the child? Blast the guy in front of him?"

"No, I got this. As soon as I cut power take the shot. Meet me back at the car." And with that he took off, running towards the house.

The gangster, meanwhile, was in a bedroom talking to a boy of maybe six, who was standing in front of him. The boy looked like a local, he was thin with dark smooth skin. He looked afraid of the gangster, but was listening to him as he spoke. The gangster seemed to be trying to coax him. I knew I didn't want to see what could happen next.

I looked on Ravi's laptop knowing he had hacked the security system. He set it to a loop so they couldn't see him coming, but as soon as power was cut, they may be alerted. I would need to be quick and accurate.

Two minutes had passed. *Come on, Ravi.*

The little boy walked closer to the gangster. If I took the shot, he would be covered in gore. This can't happen this way.

I heard Ravi radio me quietly, "Ten seconds til the power goes."

The boy sat down next to the gangster on the bed.

"Wait! The boy is on the bed!"

"No, it needs to happen now. Five seconds."

The gangster stood up and started to undo his pants. They dropped to the floor.

Right on cue, the lights cut, and I instantly took the shot. I watched the body drop and within seconds saw the familiar outline of Ravi through the infrared scope grabbing the boy and running at full sprint.

I disassembled the rifle as quickly as I could and fit all our equipment into the backpack. I jogged back to the car and reached the trunk just as Ravi burst through the woods carrying the child and completely out of breath. "Get in the back with him, I'll drive," I told him. He agreed, and sat in the backseat soothing the terrified little boy, who was sobbing, while I drove to an abandoned church, I had seen about ten miles back. I called my UN contact who agreed to meet us there. "Just stay safe in the meantime, there's a lot happening out there tonight," she warned me. *If you only knew*, I thought. We parked behind the church, hidden from the main road and waited. I looked back to find Ravi stretched out asleep with the boy sleeping peacefully on his chest. It was a heartbreaking image, I wished in that moment I could photograph them. Ravi's strong arms wrapped around this tiny little body, protecting him even in his sleep with the boy's thin arms tucked under him, his little hands, on Ravi's chest. It made me think of when Ethan was little and liked to nap with me on the couch while Jenna took her nap. Then I thought of Ravi holding his own little Nera in this same way and began to wonder if becoming a father had made him even more equipped to do this job.

I saw headlights and quickly put on my face covering and drew my weapon. My contact stepped out of the car, so I holstered my gun and gently picked the boy up from Ravi's embrace. When I handed him over to her, she said, "You guys made a huge delivery today, I can't thank you enough." I only nodded and got back in the car. I watched her leave with the boy, wondering what his future would look like, how much trauma he had already endured, if he would ever be able to live a normal life again. As Ravi slept, I sat in the car and sobbed. I cried for every child that would never be the same and wondered if what we were doing really made a difference when it comes to injustice when the injustice had already been done. I wanted it all to just stop so we didn't have to do this and children didn't have to suffer and could just have happy lives; taking naps and sharing animal cookies with their mamas on happy, lazy, weekends.

After about ten minutes, I pulled myself together and drove us back to the cottage. I roused Ravi and we both lumbered into our rooms and slept hard.

Punta Cana

We had become tourists again, waiting in the airport for our flights, drinking some awful fruity drinks and laughing about some of the "touristy" moments we experienced this vacation. The conversation was light and lively, a reward for another smooth operation complete.

"So, when do you pick up Nera?" I asked curiously.

"Next week her mother will bring her to me. I miss her terribly, I only hope that awful family didn't spoil her too much," he said looking away.

"Like you don't already," I quipped.

He smiled broadly and took a moment to answer that. "This love I have for her; I can't put it into words. You know I've always adored women, but usually temporarily. This love," he put his fist to his chest, "this is forever. I never thought that would happen to me."

"Parenthood changes us. I remember when Ethan was born, it was like a light shone down from heaven and said, 'This is your purpose'. I just knew that I would do anything for him. Same goes for Jenna. It's a different world," I looked away, a little embarrassed about being so personal about my children.

"I can honestly say I understand now." He was silent for a long time after that.

"Looks like it's time," he said.

"Yes, it is. Well, it's been a pleasure, Ravi."

"Indeed, goodbye Emelia."

We gave each other the usual end-of-mission handshake and walked our separate ways. For the first time, in the three years we had been working together, I turned to look back and was surprised to find that he had looked back, too.

5
January 2018
Hanover, New Hampshire

Work was really beginning to take off. I was teaching a full load of courses, was named Chair of the Department, and had started collaborating with some other faculty on research for my next book. It was a multi-disciplinary approach so there were several different departments contributing, it was a pretty big project for the university. We were looking at geographic factors of sex trafficking in the US and trying to make comparisons between the biggest hotspots so we could identify steps for law enforcement to minimize risks in those places. It was similar to my Reporting Initiative, but with geography. My agent wanted to market it as a textbook as well, to start branching out and reaching an entirely new market: criminology. Surely by this time next year I would be tenured and that felt great.

A sociology professor I was collaborating with stopped by my office, "Hey, how was Thailand?" Dr. Jonathan Grant played a pretty important role on my research team and we had spent hours working through the details of this research.

"Thailand was nice, very relaxing," I said. It really was fantastic, though, but the relaxing part was a lie. Ravi and I added an extra week to our operation and took down four establishments in total. We nailed down the perfect technique for how they had things set up in Thailand and just replicated it four times. We rescued three hundred and seventy-five women and children, our biggest number to date, and rid the world of thirty-three scumbag pimps. We drank champagne on the beach until the sun came up on our last night in the country, laughing and arguing and just reveling in our success.

"Sounds fun, I've always loved to travel," Jonathan said with a smile. "The team is headed to Tony's for lunch, care to join us?" He ran a hand over his trendy short beard. Between the beard, his hip rectangular glasses, and his full head of dark brown hair, he looked much younger than he was, and the students all adored him. Especially the women.

"Sure, let me grab my coat," I said. He helped me put on my coat and we walked to the parking lot. "Want to just ride with me?" he asked.

I considered this for a moment. Why not? "Sure."

He opened the passenger door of his Prius for me and off we went. We talked a little about the research on the way when the conversation wandered into personal lives. His son was graduating high school this year but lived in New York with his ex-wife and went to a private school, which he opposed because it was too "elitist". He asked about Ethan and Jenna and their school activities and responded with genuine interest; most peoples' eyes glaze over if you talk too much about kids, but he really liked to hear about them.

Tony's was a popular place for students and faculty, but someone had thought ahead to reserve a table and Jonathan and I were the last to arrive. He pulled out my chair for me and took a seat next to me. The group was excitedly discussing the criminology side of the project and were arguing over which criminology professor would be best suited to teach a class on this subject.

"Wait, I thought I was teaching this class?" I joked.

The team laughed, someone chimed in, "Yes, with all your

knowledge and experience with the criminal element of trafficking," with a sarcastic smile. I covered my mouth to stifle a laugh.

Jonathan cleared his throat, "The criminal element is only half the problem, if there wasn't a market for it there wouldn't be a problem." Hmm... he had a good point.

"No," said a very outspoken psychology instructor. "If there is no market the demand will eventually stop. These criminals need to be stopped and honestly I couldn't care less if they were all shot dead". She folded her arms across her chest to show she meant business. This conversation suddenly became *very* interesting.

"Agreed," our research assistant said. "There is no place for perverts in this world. We need a little vigilante justice and people will get the point."

Yes. I thought. *Exactly. Send a message.*

"No." Jonathan suddenly became very firm and pedantic. "If society agrees that someone shouldn't exist because of their actions there will be anarchy. There is no place in civilized society for vigilante justice, we have the justice system for that. It would be murder, plain and simple and the murderers would be no better than the criminals. People can't just take it into their own hands, they just can't!"

Someone else butted in, "But the justice system..."

The food arrived, just in time to save us from what could have been a very intense argument. We finished lunch all talking casually about lighter topics. As we left the restaurant, the wind had picked up and had a chill to it. Jonathan offered me his arm during the walk to the car, a very old-school but gentlemanly thing to do, so I accepted. He settled me into his car and when we reached the parking lot, he put the car in park and paused. He nervously adjusted his bowtie, which he had a penchant for wearing.

Uh oh.

"We should do this again some time, Emelia," he said gently. He looked at me expectantly, blue eyes shining.

"That would be nice," I offered. It sounded like a hypothetical offer anyway, so what was the harm?

"Great! How about Friday?" he suggested. "There's a fantastic piano player at The Brook and they have a huge selection of craft beers. I can make us a reservation, if you would like." He was smiling with a little color in his cheeks. Was he nervous?

"That sounds lovely," I answered. And that's how I began my first dating experience since my divorce and my second dating experience with any man.

2018

El Paso, TX

The plane touched down in El Paso and I could almost feel the heat already. Since the kids and I were going back to Kansas for summer break to visit with family and my agent was expecting me to tour with the book, Ravi and I had agreed to a short Spring Break vacation in Mexico. This was our redemption for our first botched mission, and Ravi, hating failure, had zeroed in on a specific group and their transport schedule to the United States. They used the cover of a commercial trucking business and had been taking people both to and from the US for years. This mission was simple and short, with minimal risk so I felt pretty confident as I met him in the terminal.

"Emelia."

"Ravi."

We shook hands and made our way to the car rental kiosk.

Ravi had found us a terrific condo for the week in a nicer part of El Paso. "You deserve only the best, my dear," he joked as we carried our gear and suitcases into the condo. He seemed in especially good spirits, showing me photo after photo of Nera. Here she's riding a tricycle, here she is eating ice cream, here she is reading a book with me and she recognizes all the letters because she's tremendously gifted. His ardor for this child was endless, but I wasn't really all that surprised since Ravi does everything with ardor.

We laid out our equipment and began our usual routine, discussing the plan, silently cleaning weapons. When I started really grilling him about plan details, he put down the photos and groaned. "Mia, Mia, relax. I know exactly what you need." He stared at me seriously.

"What do I need?" I asked, meeting his gaze.

"Tacos. Authentic tacos."

So, we left the condo and got tacos. Turns out he was right after all.

Juarez, Mexico

"The audacity of this group," Ravi complained as we drove through Juarez in a $300 car Ravi had bought off a kid in El Paso. "They fill a truck with people they actually kidnapped and drive it straight through the gates to the United States posing as commercial drivers. And nobody does a thing about it!" He shook his head angrily. I fanned myself and agreed, the car had no air conditioning and the heat seemed to inflame his anger. "We stop the truck in this area," he pointed to the map I was holding at a somewhat uninhabited area, "and take the truck before they can even get close to the border. Then, my favorite part, we simply take the side roads and drive the truck across the border into the US! We sneak them in, and they are none the wiser. You linked up with your people, right?"

My usual contacts for foreign operations were really of no use to me in the US. There was too much red tape to accomplish anything, so I found an unaffiliated group that was a little grittier and willing to take a few risks. "We're using Operation Underground Railroad this time. They'll meet us at the water treatment plant and take the truck from there," I said. He smiled. "Then we take the rental from there and drive back to the condo for more tacos!" He seemed very confident in the simplicity of this mission.

"How are we stopping the truck?" I asked. He mentioned that earlier, but I forgot to ask the details and now I was concerned.

"You leave that to me. I have a new gadget, it emits an EMP that disables the vehicle then I replace one of the fuses, which will take no time at all, and we continue on our way." He always had all the good gadgets.

We waited at the rendezvous point, hidden behind some mesquite trees while Ravi checked the tracer on the truck to see where it was. "Thirty seconds," he whispered. I crouched down, ready to act quickly. Headlights illuminated the road in front of us, then dimmed and we heard the truck come to a stop, completely disabled. Before the truck even stopped moving, I was quietly moving quickly toward the passenger door of the cabin. I knelt down just to the rear of the door, and as soon as it opened, I yanked a man to the ground and fired on him three times. I crept around the front of the truck and saw the driver on the ground, also dead. Ravi opened the hood of the truck and started working while I watched the road for any oncoming traffic. He was right, it was less than thirty seconds and the headlights flashed back on and he slammed the hood. "We're back in business," he said and jumped into the driver's seat while I jumped in the passenger's seat. As he eased the truck back onto the road, I smiled at him and he grinned. Like clockwork.

We drove in silence for a few minutes when I asked, "Ravi, are we murderers?"

"What? No, no, no, what we do is not murder. We are killers, yes, but not murderers." He looked at me incredulously.

"What's the difference? We take lives." I said.

"The difference is we take lives from people who deserve to die and give life to people who deserve to live. How many lives have we saved? Do you know the new thing is selling these people," he gestured to the back of the truck, "for organ harvesting? From live human beings! Human trafficking is a disgusting crime, we make the world a better place." He nodded firmly at this.

"But who are we to determine who should live and die? I mean, it is a little barbaric, this vigilante justice thing," I suggested.

"Barbaric? Emelia, if we let the powers that be handle these situations nothing would happen. Hundreds of thousands of children go missing every year and we both know exactly where they end up and when they finish with them, they die. That's barbaric. And the justice system? Law enforcement? They can't act on this like we do, the perpetrators are released as quickly as they are arrested. It is slow, corrupt, ineffective, and cruel. They don't do anything substantial. We saw that something needed to be done and we did it. We did *something*." We rode in silence for a few minutes.

"Are you feeling guilty?" he asked gently.

"No, not at all," I responded.

"Where is all this 'murderer' business coming from? An

existential crisis?" he laughed.

"Jonathan said vigilante justice makes the murderer as bad as the perpetrator and I just wanted your opinion about that and about what we do," I said. I realized my mistake too late.

"Wait, who's Jonathan?" I grabbed onto the dash as he maneuvered the truck off the highway and onto a dirt road.

"He's a sociology professor I'm working with on the book."

"Why do you care what he thinks? Is he your boyfriend?" he smirked. I *loathed* the word "boyfriend", and he knew it.

"No! I mean, we've been on a few dates but that's it."

His eyes widened at this revelation. "A few dates, huh? Like two?"

"Umm... maybe eight. Something like that." I braced for a big bump in the road, for which Ravi did not slow down.

"So, you're sleeping with him."

"No! Of course not!" I blushed at the thought.

"Liar. It's been eight dates, of course you're sleeping with him," he looked over at me mischievously.

"Ravi, I dated Bryce for two years before we had sex. It's not uncommon."

"Sure, but with other men did you wait *eight dates*?"

I looked out the window and said nothing.

His eyebrows shot up, "Dr. Emelia Burke, have you really only had sex with one man in your entire life?" He burst out laughing.

"Don't laugh at me!" but I was laughing with him. I suppose it was unusual for a woman my age.

Ravi killed the headlights as we approached the turnoff for the border. We parked briefly and scanned the area with our infrared scopes, but it looked clear. "Hold on," he said, and he drove the truck through a small clearing. The river was mostly dry and the trucks tires were in good shape so the crossing at this point was no trouble. The truck bumped and bounced as though the border were a raised line on a map, but we ended up on a dirt road adjacent to a large rectangular pond. This must be the water treatment plant.

Slowly, we drove to the north side of the pond and waited. True to their word, my contact flashed their headlights just a few yards away from us. We pulled down our face coverings and jumped out of the truck. Two large armed men walked toward us with their weapons at the ready. "Show us the contents," one of them insisted.

"No, show us your credentials first," I countered. Caution and thoroughness were necessary when you are delivering a truck full of people to strangers.

They brought out badges showing their affiliation with the group and the names matched those my contact said would be there.

I escorted them to the back of the truck and opened the door and gasped before I could stop myself. It was a full-sized commercial trailer completely filled with people. They all looked terrified, as though we were about to shoot them. Women were holding children tightly as they cried, and when the men saw us, some of them stood up, prepared to protect their families as best they could. I'm sure we appeared a little intimidating with the guns, Kevlar vests, and face coverings, and the sight of these men prepared to fight for their families made my heart ache for them.

"How many?" one of the men asked in amazement while the other spoke to them in Spanish, reassuring them that they would be safe from here.

"I have no idea," said Ravi, finally able to speak after the shock of seeing the sheer quantity of people. This was easily our biggest rescue.

"We'll take them from here," the smaller man said. "This is life-changing, for these people, you know that right? Like, you just literally saved their lives."

I gawked at him for a moment. There was nothing I could say to that. Ravi shook their hands and we started walking to the area where we stashed the rental car. As we were putting our gear in the trunk for the drive back to the condo, Ravi shook his head and laughed. "One man. Just one man in your whole life."

I rolled my eyes, "Really?" He just shrugged, laughed, and started up the car.

6
Summer 2018
Pratt, Kansas

The rest of the semester flew by in a blur. The book was finished, the tour booked, finals completed. Jonathan and I had been pretty busy, but we had a few dates (and a few steamy kisses on the porch) but he was, ever the gentleman, and ever patient. The kids and I had flown into Wichita, Kansas and rented a car to take to visit Grandma and Papa on the family farm. As we pulled up the dusty road leading to the house, we saw them waiting on the wide front porch adorned with a big, waving, American flag. Jenna and Ethan hugged them excitedly and Mom and Dad both grabbed me in a hug, catching me off guard. They were always there for me, never missed a graduation or awards assembly, but they were always short on affection and compliments. They were wonderful parents, supportive but stoic. Classic Midwestern.

This trip seemed to be exactly what the family needed. Mom taught Jenna how to make her top-secret banana bread and let her help feed the chickens. Dad taught Ethan how to drive a stick shift in his old farm truck, patiently instructing him as he grinded through the gears learning how to operate the clutch. And we all took a few trips down to the pond to do some serious fishing, which the kids quickly became obsessed with, rising early with Papa to "get the good ones". Jonathan sent me weekly texts saying, "I miss you!" or "Hope you're having fun!" to which I usually responded with a simple, "Thanks" or "I miss you, too". He was nothing if not reliable. I took a trip into town each day we were there to spend a couple hours with Grandpa, who was in Serenity Hills Nursing Home where we would watch his favorite shows, play some vicious games of gin rummy, and let him show me off to all his friends. I pushed him around the grounds of the home, where they had beautiful flower gardens and he told me stories about my grandma Rose and the war. Sometimes he called me Rose when I came to visit, but he usually realized his mistake later. He was still in good spirits and seemed as healthy as one could hope for.

For the Fourth of July, Mom and I took a trip to town to visit a cool, little antique shop while the kids helped Dad in the garden. The shop was amazing, with quaint little trinkets, vintage signs, refurbished furniture, the works. I found a fantastic dining room table but decided on some simple décor for the kitchen and the kids' rooms. We took our treasures to the counter and I recognized the woman at the counter as a girl from high school. Being a small town, everyone knew everyone, so she immediately recognized me.

"Emelia! Long time no see! How ya been?" she asked as she was ringing up our bill.

"Great! Living in New Hampshire now, just came down for a visit. How are you?" I tried to match her enthusiasm, but it wasn't easy.

"Doing good, kids are good, Tom is working down at the lumber yard, he's management now. How's Bryce doing?" I cringed at the question.

"He's good." I replied, trying to avoid it.

"Did he come, too?" she asked, looking around for him.

"No, we divorced." I stated plainly.

"Oh, I'm sorry. That's such a shame. How are the kids?" She looked at me sympathetically.

"The kids are great!" I wanted to leave. She finished bagging up our treasures in awkward silence then before we left, she grabbed my hand and said, "Take care", very sincerely.

On the trip back to the farm, Mom was chatting away pleasantly about some local gossip, but I barely heard a word she said. I was infuriated. I was a combat veteran with a PhD about to tour with my second book, but I get sympathy from people because I'm a divorced single mom? I didn't want anyone's pity and I didn't need it. I vaguely heard the end of one of Mom's stories, then, "Emelia, are you ok?"

"Yeah, just kind of zoned out for a minute." I needed to shake off this anger before seeing the kids, so I listened to Mom's gossip until we reached the farm. Dad and the kids had brought in a huge harvest from the garden, so Mom made big salads and fried squash while Dad grilled steaks and it was all delicious. We sat at the picnic table out back while we ate, then Dad brought out a huge watermelon and sliced it up for us. The town put on a big fireworks' show at the lake right next to the farm so we were able to eat our fresh watermelon and have front row seats to the finest fireworks show in the county. *This is what I needed*, I thought as I saw the kids' faces light up with each burst of fireworks.

On our last day at the farm, Dad took the kids to town to find some peaches at the farmer's market and I drank coffee at the kitchen table while Mom made biscuits for breakfast.

"I see you still wear Grandma's locket. I'm glad to see that," Mom said as she sifted flour into the mixing bowl.

"Yep, every day," I leaned over to show her the pictures of Jenna and Ethan as babies.

"Aw, I loved those pictures. You know, your Grandma wore that every day until she died. She had a picture of me and Uncle

Jim on one side and Dad on the other. You always reminded me of her. She was so tough," she continued as she mixed the dough. "She made us nice clothes from basically nothing just so we would never know how poor we were. She only had two dresses, but we always had school clothes. She was tough like you. But you seem different this time," she didn't look at me as she said this, just continued mixing the dough.

"Different? How so?"

She plopped the dough on the table and grabbed a rolling pin. "You seem more relaxed. You were always wound so tight, so worried about everything. I think it might be because you finally ditched Bryce."

Wait, what? I thought. "You weren't disappointed that I divorced?" I was shocked. No one divorced in my family, we didn't even *talk* about it, much less do it.

"Ha! When I told your dad the news he said, 'It's about damn time!' He is a good man, but he wasn't for you, Emmy." She pointed the rolling pin at me. "Let me tell you something, some men suck the strength right out of you and some men make you stronger. If you can't find one that makes you stronger, you're better off doing it by yourself." She started rolling out the dough.

I thought about this and took a sip of coffee. "And which one is dad?"

She smiled. "We've been married forty-five years, I'll let you figure that out."

I laughed and thought about mad bringing out the strength in my mother. It made me think of their relationship in a whole new light. Dad always worked so hard for our family and mom always kept the home. I imagined them working together to figure out how to make our family work, it may have been the first time I saw their relationship through adult eyes.

"What I'm trying to say is Dad and I are awfully proud of you," she cut the dough into perfect circles as she talked. "You raised two wonderful kids, made a success of yourself, and never let anything stop you. I'm... I'm just proud of you."

Tears began to well up in my eyes hearing this from my mother, so I took a drink and rinsed out my coffee mug so she couldn't see them. We aren't a crying family. When I turned around, she gave me a big hug, wiped a tear away from her own eye quickly and said, "Now, grab that package of sausage out of the fridge. I know y'all don't cook much up north but let's see if you remember how to make some good gravy for these biscuits."

I did as I was told and grabbed the flour and milk. Some things you just never forget.

San Francisco

The book tour was nothing like I expected. When I toured with my first book, my audience was familiar, other psychologists or mental health workers who were familiar with and agreed with the subject matter. There was a meeting of minds at these engagements which was very empowering. This tour, however, I struggled pitching the book to the criminal justice side of academia and even more so with law enforcement. At every stop I got the same condescending questions that came from not spending twenty years on the force; "And why do you think these methods will work when you have no experience in apprehending criminals?" I would clench my fists and think of the hundreds of criminals I've dispensed with my own hands and answer, "I believe the data speaks for itself." Some officials would even say they had a good handle on trafficking in their city already, since they apprehended six traffickers last year alone.

Only six? We do that in less than 30 minutes, I thought angrily. Ravi was right, the bureaucracy of the system slowed the work.

The last stop of the tour was in San Francisco where we were meeting with a textbook distributor over dinner to discuss and finalize our deal. I was in my hotel room putting the finishing touches to my lipstick when I got a text message:

How can the Sabbath plant a huge and shining flower in a blind and narrow heart? How can the Sabbath plant the bud of angels in a heart of raving flesh? — Zelda

I didn't recognize the number but knew immediately it was Ravi, Zelda was his favorite poet. We never sent text messages since they're so easy to trace, it was very unusual. I checked the time; it was about three in the morning in Jerusalem, so I guessed he was drunk and having an existential crisis of his own. I made a mental note to ask about it in our next email exchange and slipped my phone in my purse as I rushed out the door. Not responding to that text message was a mistake that I would come to deeply regret later.

Fall 2018

Hanover, New Hampshire

Jonathan and I had several more dates during the fall and it seemed this was becoming an actual relationship. There was no official declaration or anything, but it had been eight months and we had lunch together almost every day. One Friday afternoon I was researching Honduras and he popped his head in my office, "Please tell me you don't have plans tomorrow, we just *have* to go see this cool jazz fusion band playing at the Apple Festival downtown," he pleaded.

I actually did have plans; I had been neglecting my training a little, so I planned to spend a few hours at the range then hit the mats for some more grappling time. I looked at Jonathan, his tidy button up shirt and pressed khaki skinny pants, his hopeful smile.

If I was going to really make an effort at this, perhaps it's time to open up a little. "I do have plans, but you can join me if you'd like," I offered.

He walked in and sat on my desk, "Sure, what's the plan?"

"We can go to the range together."

"You mean the driving range? I didn't know you play golf," he said, confused.

"No, no, the shooting range. Do you have a firearm?"

His chest puffed up a little, "I keep a Glock 19 for home defense."

"Great! Bring it and pick me up at ten tomorrow morning, we can make a day of it," I said, feigning enthusiasm.

"Ok, this could be fun. Different, but fun. See you tomorrow," He leaned in for a quick kiss and was out the door. I sighed. I thought about what my mother said about men for a few minutes before closing down my computer and leaving for the evening.

I started getting my equipment ready at nine, since there was a lot of modification to do. I removed all the silencers, scopes, and replaced the trigger assembly in my AR-15 to make it back into a semi-automatic. I made sure each weapon was clean and my range bag didn't have any unusual weapons or spent brass. I left the regular scope on the AR-10, but wasn't sure if Jonathan was ready to see that side of me yet. I packed it in the bag anyway, threw on a tank top and cargo pants and tucked my usual 9mm into its holster. Jonathan arrived promptly at ten and his eyes widened slightly when I put my range bag in the trunk. "You bringing an arsenal?" he joked. I just laughed as we drove to the range.

"Morning, Emelia, the usual?" asked Don, the owner, as he stood behind the counter.

"Morning, Don, the usual but with two shooters," I said. He paused, raised an eyebrow at me and slid the key to the range across the counter. I gave him a look that made him laugh as I took the key and walked to the back where the shooting lanes were set up. Jonathan followed, fumbling with his ear protection.

The range was usually empty this time of day, which is why I usually liked this time frame. We put on our ear and eye protection and he pulled out his Glock and a couple magazines. I had four pre-loaded, so while he loaded, I emptied a mag neatly into the chest of the target. He looked at the target and back at me with wide eyes. "Nice grouping," he said casually. He took his stance and slowly emptied his magazine. We pushed the toggle to bring the target in and I noticed his grouping was shifted to the right.

"I'm no expert or anything, but if you adjust your finger on the trigger, and squeeze more gently, you'll have more accurate grouping," I suggested. He thanked me for the advice and tried again, this time with a little more accuracy. I did a quick-fire drill going from head to chest as quick as I could and he seemed shocked, but in a good way.

"This is fun!" he said.

"Yeah?" He liked it?

"Yeah!" He really did seem to be enjoying himself.

"Want to see something cool?" I asked excitedly.

"Sure," he watched me pull my AR-15 out of the bag. He took a step back and said, "What do you need that for?"

"Just watch, it's fun!" I toggled the new target further back. I popped in a magazine, pulled the charging handle and tucked the buttstock into my shoulder as I flipped the safety. It surprised me how loud it was without the suppressor, but I was still able to get clean shots. This was easily one of my favorite weapons, so I was excited.

I pulled the target in and replaced it quickly. Jonathan watched me warily as I handed him the weapon. "It doesn't have much recoil, seriously, and I chambered the first one for you already so just flip the safety and you're good to go," I said, naturally slipping into military lingo.

He looked at me uncertainly but pulled the rifle up to his shoulder and tried to mimic my stance. I could tell before he fired the first round that his shoulder would be bruised from not tucking it in, but I didn't want to seem too critical. He fired off a couple rounds and said, "Yeah, that's really cool!" He set the weapon down gently. I looked at him quizzically, picked it up and finished off the magazine, dropped the mag, and cleared it.

"Don't worry, ammo is cheap, we can shoot as much as you want," I assured him.

"Emelia, it's not about that, its—"

"Now check out this bad boy, the Valkyrie!" I set the bipod on my sniper rifle and sat down to get good positioning. I toggled the target out as far as it would go and fired off three rounds swiftly. One to the head, two to the chest, perfect. I looked back at Jonathan, and he was a little pale and stepping back.

"Jonathan? Are you ok?"

"Is that a *sniper rifle*?" he asked disgustedly.

"Yes. Is that a problem?" I asked defiantly.

"Why in the hell would you need a sniper rifle? And why are you so good at it? I mean, we work at a University for goodness sake," he said, as if it made any sense at all.

"Does it scare you?" I asked indignantly.

"Hell yes, Emelia, I mean… who the hell are you? I really thought I knew you." He stalked out of the range and waited in the car.

Stunned, I collected my gear, said goodbye to Don, and got in the car for an awkward and quiet ride back to the house. I waited for him to say something to officially end things but he simply said, "Goodbye, Emelia," and that was enough for me to know that this was over.

"Goodbye, Jonathan," I said coolly. He drove away.

Some men suck the strength right out of you and some men make you stronger.

7
December 2018
Honduras

The ocean once again had me mesmerized as I waited in the airport bar for Ravi. I chose a table next to the window for this exact reason, feeling soothed by the constancy of the waves as they broke on the white sandy beach. Looking around for Ravi, I tapped my fingers on the table, whistling along with the Neil Diamond song playing quietly in the background. A man I didn't recognize sat across from me.

"Emelia."

My jaw dropped. He had cut his hair military short and looked about five years older than the last time I saw him. He had even lost some weight. Something major had changed about him, I started to worry.

"Ravi, your hair…"

"Yes, I know, I cut it off," he said curtly, running his hand over his head quickly. He pulled out the satellite photos and immediately began briefing me on the mission. He had done much more extensive research than usual, so I had very little to contribute to the briefing. He had the entire mission planned from start to finish.

"Well, it looks like you stole my thunder this time," I said with a laugh.

He nodded but said nothing.

"What is going on? Are you ok?" I was really starting to worry about him, everything was off about him.

"Let's go meet with the group and get this over with," he muttered and walked quickly in the direction of the terminal. I practically had to jog to keep up with him.

When the group arrived, he put on a little more of an act to pretend to be normal, but it wasn't very convincing. We all settled into the resort and met for dinner to do our usual catch up.

Of course, Mark and Julia filled us in on all the details of their life, leaving very little out. It took them a while, so we had enough time to start to relax from the drinks. Diana, the Australian woman, told us all about her budding photography business, and the McBride's, a couple from Texas, announced their pregnancy, which led to a joyous toast and many congratulations.

"Speaking of babies, how is that darling child of yours, Ravi?" asked Julia.

He cleared his throat and looked at his hands in his lap. "She was killed in a rocket attack six months ago."

The entire table gasped... then silence. Ravi wouldn't lift his head, and nobody knew how to express condolences for something so tragic. My heart sank and I felt tears stinging my eyes.

Ravi whispered, "Pardon me," and walked away from the table toward the beach. I started to follow, but Diana jumped up and followed quickly to console him. In his absence, half the table cried and expressed condolences like, "Oh, poor Ravi! That sweet little child!" and "Such a tragedy, it's a shame" and "We should cheer him up this week". I couldn't stand it any longer. I excused myself and went up to my room. I looked out the window and saw Diana sitting next to him on the beach with her arm around his shoulders. He only stared into the ocean. I sighed and laid down on my bed and cried myself to sleep.

Normally, during tourist week, Ravi and I run every morning. We run in silence, but there's a competitive edge to it. Since he's about seven inches taller than me I have to push myself hard to keep up with him and he never relents on his pace. After the run, there is usually an all-out sprint followed by playful razzing over who had the quicker time while we stretch. After everything that played out the night before, I expected to run alone that morning. I rose at 0530 and took the elevator to the lobby and as the door opened, there Ravi stood, in running clothes.

"You ready?" he said.

"Yes."

We stretched on the beach in silence and began to run. It was just like normal, except there was no edge to it, he was running at my pace. After a few miles I noticed out of the corner of my eye that there were tears streaming down his face as he ran. We ran ten miles that morning, stretched in silence and went back to our rooms. We ran ten miles in the same manner every day of tourist week, I think it was the closest we came to truly confronting the horror he had been through in the last six months.

The rest of the week, I rarely saw him. He spent most of the week lounging on the beach with Diana, who looked spectacular in a cutout one piece and a wide sunhat. I chose to see the sights with the McBride's, who were chatty enough to give me little reason to talk, which is exactly what I wanted. They were relentless tourists, wanting to see everything they could so we stayed very busy and stayed fairly isolated from the group. As the week ended, I was sad to see them go but was hoping Ravi was ready to open up a little about what happened. Or, at least, be well enough to reassure me that he was capable of performing the mission. I had my doubts.

San Pedro Sula, Honduras

Prepping for this mission was like walking on eggshells. We did our usual routine with the equipment prep, but there was no banter, no laughter. He filled me in on the details of the city, very dangerous, controlled by two gangs.

"It will be a lot like Haiti, but without inciting a gang war. We stick to one side of the city, bring the victims out the window in the front of the building onto the tin roof and down into the bus, which I've already secured. The difference is you're driving and I'm taking out the downstairs guards, eight of them. Should be pretty straightforward, but it will be a two-hour drive to the UN building so that part may be uncomfortable. But I will have a car ready for us afterward." He had nailed the mission down pretty well.

"Sounds good. So, I go high, you go low tonight?"

"You can if you want, but there's no need. The sat photos are very recent." He walked off toward his bedroom.

"Ravi, about what happened…" He stopped with his fists clenched, his back to me.

"I… I'm just so sorry. For your loss." The words felt like meaningless platitudes as I said them.

"Thank you," he said quietly. He shut the door for the night.

Mission day finally arrived, and Ravi dropped me off at the salvage yard and roared away on the motorcycle. A stout, short man met me at the gate.

"Para Ravi?"

"Si."

He nodded and drove a decommissioned city bus to the gate. He placed it in park and I got in the driver's seat. "Gracias," I told him, but he just waved a dirty hand at me as I drove into the darker part of the city. It was harder than I expected, maneuvering

82

the bus through the curving and narrow streets. Ravi always made it look easy. I approached the target with about five minutes to spare so I parked a couple of blocks away and used my scope to watch the front of the building for any unusual happenings. In truth, I wanted to see Ravi enter the house, I needed to see his demeanor to tell if this mission would go south. Right on schedule he rounded the corner and kicked in the door with his weapon drawn. All seemed normal so far. I waited until my time was up then drove the bus right beside the tin roof. I climbed on the bus and opened the window from the outside, apparently security wasn't a huge concern here.

Unlike Haiti, the upstairs was just one big room lined with mattresses with women and children sleeping. God only knows what happened in this room during the night. I roused the women, *"Ven conmigo, estoy aqui para salavarte Estaras a salvo,"* the same thing I always said to all the victims. They started moving nervously toward the window, I told them, *"Sube al bus rapido!"* or, "Get in the bus quickly". The women looked exhausted, having only just finished a night's "work" but the idea of getting out and somewhere safe energized them. There weren't as many children as in Haiti, I was grateful for that, and the women took care to get the children out first. Usually, Ravi would've radioed me that the downstairs was handled by now and would be on his way up. Something was wrong.

I found the staircase, drew my pistol and sneaked down the stairs, looking for any signs he was in distress. I saw four bodies in the living room and walked to the bedrooms, one had been shot five times, another had his throat slit. I stepped over number seven in the hall, who had half of his skull missing. This was brutal. I heard a struggle. I rushed into the back room and kicked open the door to find Ravi strangling a man with his bare hands.

83

It was clear this man had already been beaten to a pulp and was suffering. I walked over and put a bullet between the man's eyes.

"No!" Ravi screamed. "I almost had him!" His face was covered in blood, this was not the look of a tourist, he looked like a madman. This wasn't part of the plan and made things a lot more complicated.

I grabbed him by the shirt and shook him, "Get your shit together and let's get out! We have a job to do!"

This seemed to work, as he picked up his weapon and we sprinted out of the house and into the bus. It wasn't as crowded as it was in Haiti, thankfully, but it was still a good score. I drove through the streets at normal speed, trying not to draw too much attention. My scheme didn't work, four men on motorcycles flanked the bus and this time I knew they weren't there to keep us safe. I hit the gas hard, but the bus struggled to make speed and the gang members were closing in. They fired first, eliciting screams from the people on the bus.

"I got this," Ravi said and he popped open the escape hatch at the top of the bus. He stood on the backs of two seats straddling the aisle and used the hatch as a gunner's hatch, firing wildly at the gang members. Two were hit and crashed but there was one getting closer to the driver's window. I opened the window and pulled my pistol and fired twice, missing the first time, but taking out the motorcyclist's knee causing him to skid off the road. Ravi fired off a few more rounds and dropped back into the bus. "Route secure," Ravi yelled, so I eased off the gas a little. He continued to wander up the aisle of the bus, checking on the women and children and looking for more people following us. One of the women was hit with the gunfire and didn't look like she would survive, but the other women tended to her and Ravi patched her up the best he could with our limited med kit. The

84

children were crying as the women tried to soothe them and keep them away from Ravi, who looked terrifying.

Two grueling hours later we made it to about a half mile from the UN drop off point when the bus finally overheated and quit. We instructed the victims to stay on the bus and jogged to the drop point to meet the contact, with our faces covered, of course. She yelled back to her partners in Spanish and they all rushed to work. We considered our job here done and slowly walked to the stashed car about another half mile from the drop site. This walk was silent, no victory dances or granola bars. Just Ravi covered in blood and me wondering what the hell was going on.

"Take off your shirt," I told him back at our safe house.

"No."

"Take off your shirt now. I need to look at your injuries." Blood was now pouring off him, it couldn't be all from the slaughter at the pimp house.

Ravi sighed. He knew this was a battle he wouldn't win. He took off his shirt and I found four deep knife slashes on his forearms and a gunshot wound to his bicep. How he could be so calm with these kinds of injuries, I don't know, but I grabbed the full med bag and told him to sit. And he obeyed.

I went to the kitchen for supplies and started back to the table but turned and grabbed a bottle of tequila from the freezer. I started to draw up the anesthetic before I pulled the bullet out and he insisted, "No anesthetic." I thought so.

"Fine." I said angrily and slammed the bottle of tequila down on the table next to him. He waited a moment, then opened it and took a long swig.

The repairs of all his wounds took some time to do properly, this was also the first time I had pulled a bullet from him, but he sat still during all of it and never complained about the pain. He

85

just drank the tequila like water, so by the time I had cleaned him up, bandages applied, and a shot of antibiotics administered he was tremendously drunk. Usually, when Ravi would drink, he would talk nonstop but not this time. He maintained that eerie silence that characterized this whole mission. I had to help him get to his bed and undress him. I thought he was asleep already, so I covered him with the blanket, hesitated, then kissed his forehead. He grabbed my hand as I was walking out.

"Please, Mia, will you sleep next to me?"

I didn't say a word, just stripped down to my tank top and panties and crawled into bed next to him. He fell asleep instantly. I laid next to him for an hour, thinking about sweet Nera, the pain he has lived with for six months, the suffering. He sobbed in his sleep a couple of times, and I soothed him by rubbing his back until he fell asleep again. Finally, the exhaustion took me, and I fell asleep, too.

La Ceiba Airport

The wait for our flights was painfully uncomfortable. Ravi, hungover, slumped in his seat wearing sunglasses and complaining about the heat. I had no words for him. He compromised the mission on one hand, but he also just suffered a great loss. I felt both anger and compassion toward him and had no idea how to express it, so I said nothing. They called for boarding on my flight, so I stood up.

"Ravi."

"Emelia."

We shook hands, but he never stood up. I walked away and looked back, but he didn't look, just hung his head.

8
Spring 2019
Hanover, New Hampshire

"Like this, mom?" Jenna asked, then expertly threw her brother over her hip and onto his back.

"Exactly! Know your center of balance then use their weight against them, most people you'll fight will be bigger than you, so you have to be ready for that," I said. Although she still had the face of a pre-teen, especially with the braces, her body was growing, and her figure was almost identical to mine. She needed to learn that having breasts and a different center of balance changed the way you have to fight if she was going to earn her black belt next week. Ethan had already earned his, studying and practicing with discipline. Jenna, on the other hand, wasn't as precise as Ethan but she did everything with more grit. She scared her opponents when she sparred because she always wanted to win.

Ethan jumped up and started showing her another move, so I jogged inside to grab us all drinks. As I walked by my phone, I heard the email notification. I glanced at it, and it was Ravi doing a "travel group" check in and planning our next destination. I had been researching some lower-level missions, unsure of his emotional stability after what happened in Honduras, but when I opened the email, he asked me how I felt about going to Dubai. I sent him a reply using our normal codes:

Dubai seems a little posh for the group we go with. Rich and elite, isn't really our thing. Isn't there somewhere a little more low key?

--E

He replied instantly:

Don't worry, there's some old-world charm in some of the neighborhoods. And plenty of culture. Trust me on this one.

--R

I wasn't sure how much I could trust him at this point. One of his most useful traits on these missions was his stability and our ability to read each other. I'm not sure either of those were still there. But, as long as we weren't trying to take on an elite pedophile ring with a two-person team, I suppose it wouldn't be much different to the other missions.

I replied:

Ok, Dubai it is. Let the group know and let me know if I should bring anything special to get through customs (meaning, do I need any special equipment).

--E

"What's that?" Ethan asked, reading over my shoulder.

"Nothing, just going over vacation plans with the group. Dubai this summer!" I tried to sound excited.

He looked at me suspiciously. "Dubai?" He sighed, "Mom, sit down. We need to talk." I suddenly felt like he was the adult, and I was about to get lectured, but I nonetheless sat down to listen.

"You know I read your books, right?"

"You read my books? Why?" I asked, shocked.

"I was interested. I mean, you're my mom and you wrote two books, so I wanted to read them. Anyway, you did a ton of research on human trafficking. You are basically the expert on it, but what I don't understand is why you keep vacationing in all the most dangerous places for human trafficking. And, alone, as a woman! It seems like you're taking a lot of risks." This was such a bizarre conversation to be having with my seventeen-year-old son, but he made a good point. He has never been much of a risk taker, very responsible and cautious since he was a little boy.

"Ethan, you have nothing to worry about. I travel with a group I'm very familiar with and we stick to the really touristy places. They aren't that dangerous. I'm not wandering around the slums of Calcutta alone at night, it's very safe so I don't want you to worry." I felt bad being so blatantly dishonest with him, but he was my child, after all, and I needed to protect him from certain information. I grabbed his hand and squeezed giving him a reassuring smile.

He smiled back. "Ok, just be careful," and he gave me a quick hug before jogging upstairs. I looked out the patio doors and saw Jenna walking through the moves to do the hip throw, looking fierce and determined.

My worrier and my warrior, I thought to myself.

Summer 2019

I pulled my SUV into Bryce and Laura's long private driveway. He had built her an enormous house surrounded by trees right outside the city in a sleek suburb. It was one of those ultra-modern angular houses with floor to ceiling windows everywhere. *A sniper's dream*, I thought to myself but shook the thought off as I put the SUV in park.

Jenna and Ethan walked right up to the front porch when Laura came out with baby TJ toddling behind her. "EEEFAN! NENNA!" he squealed, running with chubby little outstretched arms. He really was a cute kid, and he adored the other kids. Laura watched, smiling.

"Bryce still at work?" I asked.

"Yes, should be home in about an hour," she said. It still

always felt a little awkward between just the two of us.

"Any big plans with the kids while I'm gone?" I asked.

"Washington DC, Ethan said he always wanted to go. As long as this little monster cooperates, it should be fun," she said gesturing toward TJ.

We shared a laugh at this. There's no denying, motherhood is almost always the common ground for any two women.

"Jenna used to love the little baby backpack when she was that age, it's a lot easier than a stroller, too." I suggested.

"Good idea, thanks," she gave me a genuine smile.

"Well, have fun. I'll see you in a few weeks," I said awkwardly.

"You too, be safe," she said.

I got back in the SUV feeling the familiar ache of missing the kids combined with the excitement of going on another mission. This juxtaposition always made me want to laugh and cry simultaneously. But it was time to focus. According to Ravi, I had lots of "culture" to experience.

2019

Dubai, United Arab Emirates

This was a long flight. I had several transfers, and it took almost twenty-four hours altogether. I rarely felt this exhausted after a flight but this one had really taken it out of me. I was nervous, tired, and dirty. I slowly walked through the terminal, looking for the place Ravi and I had agreed to meet so I could secure us a table. I entered the café and saw that he had already arrived. His hair was growing back, and he was leaning over some photos, circling something with a pen and looking... normal. I approached the table cautiously.

"Ravi."

"Emelia."

His eyes looked brighter than before, giving me hope. I sat down and we did a quick brief of the mission, which was surprisingly simple. It was fully collaborative, just like usual, and I felt a little more confidence in him.

"Remember when I told you I didn't want to invest in that nightclub? This is why," he said tapping the photo. "They have a legitimate club downstairs, but upstairs is where they sell the women. Or, in this case, children. I couldn't have any part of that, right there in Israel!" He shook his head. "Anyway, I'll need to do some ground recon to confirm what our intel showed us but should be, how do you Americans say, 'easy-peasy'?"

I laughed at that, hearing him say "easy-peasy" was more comforting to me than anything else I had seen already. "Yes, easy-peasy. You ready to meet with the group?" I asked. He sighed. "Yes. Let's go be tourists," he said with a slight smile.

At dinner, the conversation was cautious and awkward. No one wanted to mention children, Nera in particular, so there were a few lulls in the conversation that even a steady flow of drinks couldn't quell. The Japanese couple had begun to learn English, so Ravi engaged mostly with them and hearing him try to say Japanese phrases with his thick Israeli accent brought us all to tears with laughter. He soothed the awkwardness with his charm, that was always one of his greatest talents. Diana walked in late, tanned, and dressed in a very fitted designer dress with sky high heels. She sat across from Ravi, laughing loudly at his jokes and reaching over to touch his hand as she talked about her photography business. I rolled my eyes to myself and sipped my drink.

With that part out of the way, I was fairly certain Ravi was on the road to recovery. Satisfied with that, I excused myself early and went to my room for a long shower and some time looking at the ocean. I snuggled down in my chair and let my mind go free for a while.

The next morning Ravi met me in the lobby right on cue for our morning run. These runs throughout the week had a similar quality to our runs in Honduras, slower, no competition, starting and stopping in silence. The last day, however, Ravi started to push the pace a little. I picked it up to meet his pace, but he pushed it more. We ended the six miles breathless but feeling accomplished. As we stretched in silence, I noticed a small scar on his ankle and started to giggle.

"What's so funny," he asked as he stretched his quads.

For some reason, this turned my giggle into a full-on laugh. Breathlessly, I said, pointing at his scar, "Do you remember that time in India when the snake bit you?" and started laughing heartily again. "You were begging me for a tourniquet and sweating, saying your heart was going to explode on the way to the hospital?" I fell to the ground laughing.

Ravi looked at me with his hands on his hips, brow furrowed. "I thought I was going to die."

I continued to laugh as I said, "Do you remember the doctor? You were screaming, 'Save my leg, please!' and he was typing away on his phone?" I was almost hysterical by then.

He started to smile, "That doctor was a tool anyway."

I couldn't stop laughing, "He said, h—he said…"

Ravi stood ramrod straight and in a perfect Indian accent said, "If this is the snake that bit you it is an Indian grass snake and non-venomous. I recommend ice and ibuprofen for the swelling. Thank you very much." At his perfect imitation he fell to the ground laughing, too.

We looked like fools, sitting on the beach, laughing so hard we were crying but we really didn't care. "And you immediately stopped screaming, stood up, and walked out!" I fell back with a new wave of laughter. Ravi helped me up and we giggled the whole way to the hotel lobby. "I almost lost my life that day, Emelia, and yet you laugh!" he gave me a playful shove.

We walked through the lobby to the elevators and before I got on, Ravi suddenly swept me into a tight hug. We held each other like that for several moments, before he let go and stepped onto his elevator without a word.

That evening, the group wanted to have a beach volleyball game before our last dinner of this trip. I showed up on the beach in some jogging shorts, a sports bra, and my hair tucked through a baseball cap. Being short, I had to work harder in high school to make the volleyball team, but I made it through lots of practice and sheer determination. Julia and the Saito's decided to watch and cheer us on, my team was me, Mark, and the Johnsons, a couple from California who competed in triathlons together in their spare time. The other team was Ravi, Diana, and the McBride's. I felt pretty good about these odds and we all good-naturedly trashed talked each other as we waited for Diana to show up.

"Hey, guys!" we hear and look over to see Diana, her hair swinging over her shoulder, wearing a white string bikini. Being model thin, this left little to the imagination, though I couldn't help but think to myself that it was hardly an outfit for volleyball. Ravi let out a low whistle and the Johnson husband simply said, "Yeah, man. For real." Mrs. Johnson elbowed him hard in the ribs and glared at him, so we all moved to our side of the net to get into position. Diana piled her hair on top of her head into a perfect messy bun and the other team got into position as well.

The game was actually a lot of fun, our team was ahead by a couple of points because Mark had some serious volleyball skills, too, even at his age. Diana was tall, so she was good in front of the net, but afraid to break her nails by making a proper fist. I saw Ravi trying to show her how she could do it and still spare her nails, wrapping his hands around hers. Our cheering section was really getting into the game as well, since they had drinks flowing and it was pretty exciting. Ravi was up to serve for their team and lobbed it way beyond the boundaries. Hannah McBride gave him a hard time about it, "You would be serving a lot better if you were looking at the ball instead of Diana's booty," which elicited a laugh from everyone, especially when she gave it a little shake toward him, and he pretended to faint. I laughed along, but thought the joke was getting a little old.

Diana and I were face to face at the net, we only needed two more points and this game would be our victory and I wanted that win. Chase McBride hit a floater right over the net and I saw my chance, I jumped as high as I could and spiked the ball hard… right into Diana's face. She fell to the ground and Ravi immediately picked her up and carried her to the deck chair as she cried. Her nose was bleeding pretty profusely, so he grabbed someone's drink, grabbed the ice with his hand and held it over the bridge of her nose. She was crying about the pain, and her broken nail, everyone was standing around her trying to make it better. Offering her a towel to clean up, a bottle of water, anything she needed. Ravi soothed her, "Don't worry, I'll take you to get the finest manicure in Dubai. Don't worry about a thing, I'll take care of you."

Diana was a delicate flower of a woman and I crushed her. I never felt more like a Disney villain in my life. I was like the witch who gave Snow White the apple. I grabbed her hand and said, "I am so, so sorry. I promise I didn't mean to hit you with the ball."

She sniffed a little and said, "I know you didn't, it's ok, it just hurts so much," and started crying again. Since villains really have no place in fixing the princess, I decided to go back to my room. Mrs. Johnson gave me a wink on my way in and whispered, "Nice shot," which would normally make me laugh but at this moment made me feel even worse.

I took the elevator to my room and showered then took a long time looking in the mirror. Thanks to my mom's good genes I didn't have any gray hair yet, but as I looked closer, I saw tiny wrinkles by my eyes, some call them smile lines, but I think that's just to make us feel better about getting older. I was thirty-eight years old and anything but a delicate flower of a woman. I never had been and never would be. Perhaps that's why Bryce chose Laura. I know for a fact that's why things didn't work out with Jonathan. I put some moisturizer on my face and ordered a huge fruit platter and a Diet Coke from room service. I settled into my cushy robe and laid down for a night of watching horror movies by myself. For the first time in my life, I truly wondered where my place in the world was. And I wondered if the only place in the world for strong women is alone.

9

The new villa was perfect for the preparations we needed to do. It was private, smaller than we were used to, but had a large kitchen table for us to work on. We immediately set to work, prepping the equipment. Ravi was much more subdued than he was before, but he was still himself and I was grateful to relax into our comfortable routine. Once all the equipment was ready, we discussed the plan. "The truck is secured for the day after tomorrow, so tomorrow we review the newest sat photos and rest up, the drive only gets us partway to the contact site, so we'll have to walk the last mile or so," he said. He had done recon at the club the night before and it was just as depraved as we suspected. Western tourists knew that it was a place to find children, so they frequented it even though it wasn't in the central club district.

"This will be a big score for us, Emelia. There won't be as many, but these are mostly children. They need us the most," he said.

"I agree. That last walk will be hard for them, but I think we can do it." I absentmindedly cleaned my pistol again, the only weapon I would be taking on this mission.

"I never did get to ask, how are things with you and Dr. Sociology?" he gave me a wry smile.

"Eh, I scared him away." I walked to the kitchen, needing a drink. I grabbed a beer from the fridge.

"You? How did you manage that? Did you spike a volleyball into his face" He laughed hard at this little jab, but it stung.

"He wasn't the kind of man who makes me stronger," I said as I took a long swig from the bottle.

Ravi just nodded his head. He sat in silence for a few moments. "Emelia, why do you do this?" This question caught me off guard. Hadn't we already discussed this?

"I already told you, the internship, the children, it inspired me," I answered, feeling annoyed.

"That was the conference answer, but now I want to know the real answer. Why?" he insisted.

"I don't know, I mean, why do you do it?" I took another long drink.

He regarded me with an exasperated look, "I already told you about IDF. Tell me the real reason." I was beyond annoyed now; I felt my cheeks getting hotter. "Ravi, please."

"Were you a victim of some sort?" he asked gently.

I slammed the bottle down on the table. "No! I literally had a perfect childhood and until 9/11 had no true sense of what injustice was. But seeing those towers fall made me feel angry and helpless. So, I joined the Army in the middle of going to college to do what was right. When I was in the Army, I was actually *doing* something about that injustice. And since then? What have I done? I saw what those children went through and I wrote a fucking book. Does that do anything? Does it change anything?"

"Mia, its ok, you don't have to talk about it," he held his hands out to me calmly.

"No, you insisted. You pushed. And now we do what we do but does it stop it? It still happens everywhere! Children are exploited every day and no number of missions can change that! It's just not fair!" I was on the verge of tears but didn't want him to see so I stalked into the kitchen for another beer. I needed something stronger.

"Injustice is a part of the human condition; we can't change that. Do you think a rocket attack on a daycare is just? We have to accept that there are some things in the world we simply can't change," he sounded perfectly calm as he said this. I considered this. If we can't change that injustice what were we even doing here? Risking our lives for nothing? Nothing about that felt right.

"I refuse to accept that. We have to keep fighting until it's gone. I... I need that."

"Mia, that's impossible. We help who we can and change their lives, maybe that's the best we can do with our time on earth." How could he be so zen about all this?

I stood at the kitchen table shaking. I had always been the type who saw a problem and solved it. These missions were to serve that purpose. What had all the training been for? All the range time, jujitsu lessons, the bruised knuckles, scars, the hardness I had acquired. What was it for? I found myself feeling the weight of all the world's injustice and suddenly felt claustrophobic and too contained.

"I need some time alone," I said and stormed out of the villa. I wandered down to the beach with a small bottle of whiskey and walked along the sand, trying to think of a solution. Of course, there is no solution. So, I just sat down and watched the waves, trying not to fall apart at the meaninglessness of all the tragedies in this life.

I stumbled into the room and went straight to the kitchen for a glass of water and some ibuprofen. I was feeling a little drunk, and I hadn't been drunk in years. The room was spinning but I managed to fill a glass. I leaned against the counter, taking long sips. Ravi slipped into the kitchen and leaned against the sink directly across from me. He, too, was drinking what looked like whiskey from a glass. *Great minds think alike*, I thought groggily.

"Mia... do you feel better now?" he asked. He looked concerned.

"No."

"Do you want to talk about it?" he insisted.

"No, Ravi, I don't want to talk about it. I just want to do something about it." I threw my glass in the sink and it shattered.

He looked at the sink, looked at me, then threw his glass in the sink as well, shattering it. "Is that what you want? You want to be angry?" he was almost yelling at this point.

"No."

"Then what do you want, Mia? What do you really want?" He stared at me with a straight face. He always stayed calm in my waves of anger, somehow. I stared back at him. I knew exactly what I wanted.

I grabbed his face and kissed him, fiercely. He hesitated for just a moment, then wrapped his arms around my waist and pulled my body close to his. His kiss was passionate, yet gentle, and feeling his familiar hands on my waist in such an unfamiliar way was thrilling. I wrapped my arms around his neck as he picked me up and sat me on the countertop, grinding his hips into mine.

Suddenly, we heard a loud ding from his laptop security tracker. He pulled away just enough to whisper something in my ear in Hebrew as he caressed my hair, then rushed over to his laptop.

"Something is happening at the club, there is unusual activity. Maybe just an influx of tourists, but we can't be sure. I'm sorry, but we'll have to move the mission up to tomorrow." He looked at me reluctantly.

"Tomorrow? Are we prepared?"

"Yes, I'll let my contact know I need the truck early tomorrow morning and we'll hit the club at eight am," he was already texting furiously on his phone.

I waited for him to finish and he walked over to me slowly. I reached up and wrapped my arms around his neck, but he pulled them away. "You need sleep."

"No, I know what I need," I reached for him again.

"Not like this, Mia. You need rest." The smoldering look in his eyes said otherwise. Still, I felt rejected. I went to my room and closed the door quietly, setting my alarm and going to bed with my clothes on.

6am

Dubai

Ravi ambled out of his room shirtless, wearing only pajama pants. I stood in the kitchen reviewing the interior photos of the nightclub. I wore a long-sleeved button up blouse, cargo pants with boots, and a bright blue, fringed scarf to wrap around my head when we were in the older section of the city so I could blend in with the locals a little better. I set his coffee and bagel on the breakfast bar and went back to drinking my own coffee and looking at the photos to memorize the layout.

"Good morning," he ventured, "how are you feeling?" I could feel his eyes burning in the back of my head.

"I'm fine," I said. I was fine… physically.

"Well…" he sat down at the bar, "that's good."

We had breakfast in silence. He stood up to go get ready, paused and turned around to face me. He looked at me gently, as if I may explode at any second.

"Mia…"

"No, it's mission day. Everything is fine, I'm fine, and we have some more details to go over. I need you to focus now," I said firmly, without making eye contact.

He nodded. "Right." He stalked off to get ready and I sighed. Mission first. Always.

7am

"The owner has an apartment in the back of the club where he stays when he's in town. Can you believe it? The guy has a whole family somewhere else in the city, but he stays here on the weekends and sells children and sleeps with the women that come into the bar. He's disgusting." Ravi shook his head at this. "You will need to get into the apartment and take him out, then go out this side door and make sure the road is clear since I'm bringing them out the front door, which is a bold plan, Emelia," he smiled at me as he said that, but I just looked out the window.

Since the second half of this plan involved me waiting in the street and blending in, I was only bringing my pistol, while Ravi was carrying the usual load. I double checked the silencer as we pulled up to the house where we would pick up the truck. The unfortunate part of this plan involved meeting with our rescue contact in the only place in Dubai where we could be certain to avoid any interference: the middle of the desert. The road only went so far, then the sand made it unpassable, so we would walk the children approximately one mile to a main road where OUR (Operation Underground Railroad operatives) would be waiting. It would be a brutally hot walk, so we brought cases of water hoping it would be enough to sustain the children until they were safe.

Ravi didn't say a word as he jumped out of the car and picked up the truck. I drove a few blocks away from the club and parked the car. I took a moment before getting out, clearing my head of the previous night and focusing all my thoughts on the mission. I found myself holding my locket almost like a rosary.

Lord, protect all these children, I thought as I got out and walked toward the front door of the club. I pulled my scarf up to cover my hair and wrapped it around my neck. Moments later, Ravi rounded the corner from the alley, gave me a nod, and kicked the door in. I followed with my gun drawn. We looked around the main room of the club, which smelled like stale smoke, sweat, and vomit. *Nice place.* It was dim and dusty, there was a huge dance floor in the middle with a winding staircase on the left side of the building. We closed the door behind us, and Ravi took out his bolt cutters to cut the lock and chain securing the children upstairs while I found the door behind the DJ's booth leading to the owner's quarters.

Sneaking through the door and through a living room full of empty liquor bottles and overflowing ashtrays, I could hear the owner snoring and was filled with anger over what Ravi had told me about him. A monster like that shouldn't be allowed to sleep so soundly. This would be a very satisfying kill, indeed. I quietly opened the door to his bedroom and saw him sleeping alone, wearing only his underwear. I broke protocol and squatted next to his bed, close to his face. I could see the slight stubble growing on his jowly cheeks, the sweat gleaming on his bare back, the drool coming from his mouth as he snored. I smiled and said, "Wake up, I want you to know what's happening to you." He jerked awake, eyes wide, but before he could even lift his huge body to grab the pistol on his nightstand, I shot him in the temple, spraying blood on the pillow, letting him sleep forever.

I cleared the rest of the apartment, it was empty, and radioed Ravi that the ground floor was secure. I walked onto the dance floor of the club to see Ravi leading a group of maybe forty children down the stairs. These poor babies, they looked as young as five, were wearing makeup and suggestive clothes, even the little boys. I gawked at the sight for just a moment, then jogged to the side door to check the road. I opened the door, but instead of being met with the bright morning sunlight, I saw a winding staircase, and at the top two security guards leaning on their weapons casually. They looked as stunned as me as I fired on both of them, killing them instantly. I radioed Ravi, "Take them to the truck, there's a basement! I'm going down and I'll bring more up if I find them."

I silently descended the stairs, expecting more sleeping quarters, and reached a single door. I checked the doorknob quietly; it was unlocked so I opened it carefully to see a long room with a bed set up at the back of the room. There appeared to be a man in it with a woman (or child), but I couldn't quite tell. The room was mostly empty and some unfamiliar music was playing quietly. The man had two security guards at the far end of the room. I saw the other two, much closer, as I took one out with my pistol and kicked the other one back and swung around firing off three rounds, missing with the first two. I was in trouble and I knew it. I radioed Ravi the code word for when we needed to separate, "Romeo!" and dimly heard him start the truck upstairs. We'd had to separate before and meet up later at the rendezvous point so I knew he probably wasn't alarmed. Which is exactly what I wanted, the mission had to continue, and the children had to be delivered.

The other two guards had already pulled their weapons and were heading towards me when the man in the bed yelled, "Stop!" They stood their ground, all of us pointing our weapons at each other, and the man started to laugh. "Who would be stupid enough to send a *woman* to assassinate me?" he said with a heavy Russian accent. He gestured behind me and I felt an arm wrap around my neck. I wiggled out of my scarf and delivered a swift kick to his kneecap, sending him sprawling but the other two guards grabbed me by the arms. The man attached to the arm that had been around my neck was an enormous bald man with some kind of bird tattooed on his neck. I mentally prepared for a beating, but instead he pulled a syringe out of his coat pocket, injected my arm, and I slept.

10

"...feeling better?" The words rang in my ears. I opened my eyes, but only saw a red blur and felt my head pounding. I closed my eyes again.

My head was yanked back by my hair and I saw a flash as the left side of my face began to burn. The slap had its intended effect as I was starting to wake up a little.

"I said, are you feeling better? You would be smart to answer me when I ask you a question," the Russian growled. I tried to summon a response, but it came out as a groan.

"Good. We need to have a talk, you and I." He sat back in his chair and rubbed his head.

I tried to rub my eyes but realized my arms were stretched behind me. A plank of wood was behind my back and my hands were bound to each end of it with leather handcuffs. To my horror, I noticed I was also naked except for my black silk panties. I was on my knees on plush deep red carpet in a small room with bright wallpaper and a high ceiling. There were small end tables with fresh flower arrangements by each of the highbacked chairs that lined the walls. We definitely weren't in the club anymore.

"I'll start with the easier questions. You don't seem too bright," he tapped his head, "so I'll keep it simple. Who do you work for?" He folded his hands in his lap. He looked to be maybe fifty, and in decent shape. He also looked like he could probably hurt me, so I tried to think carefully before answering but my mind was still dulled from the drugs. I shook my head to clear my thoughts before answering and he rolled his eyes and gestured to my left. I looked over, and the brute from the club slammed his fist into my face, knocking me on my side and leaving me seeing stars.

"I know you've been following me. Weeks, maybe months. I know these things because I watch. I watch *everything,*" he gestured wildly with his hands as he said this, and I started to see that this man was deeply delusional. Which makes him even more dangerous. He paced in front of me and I tried to turn my wrists to see if I could slip out of the restraints. They wouldn't budge. "So, again, who do you work for? Is it Mikhail? The Irish? Who is it?"

"Nobody," I said thickly. Blood was starting to trickle down my nose.

"Americans! I should've known!" He clapped his hands and laughed to himself. Suddenly, he dashed across the room right in front of my face and whispered, "You're CIA, right? You put the bug in my plane, didn't you?" His eyes were wide, and he was breathing heavily. Apparently, I didn't answer quick enough because he slapped me hard, this time on the right side of my face.

"I don't know anything, and I don't work for anyone!" I screamed.

"Liar!" he roared and kicked my chest knocking me backwards.

As I tried to turn over to get up, the Russian began ranting again, half in Russian and half in English. He truly believed he was being followed all the time and that half the people working for him were double agents. He had a massively inflated sense of self-importance, which is common in patients dealing with paranoid delusions. Seeing his rant, even through the pain and the drugs, I could diagnose him already.

The Russian knelt over me, leaning close to my face again. "I know you have the answers I want. I will get what I want from you," he said gently. He traced a finger slowly down my neck making me shudder, then ripped the locket off my neck. "What have we here? Two babies? This could be fun!" He laughed and I struggled to get off my back. "Anatoly, take your time, I'll see what I can find out about these two then maybe she'll be willing to talk. Just remember, I like them broken, not dead." He stopped at the door and said, "Don't worry, my American sweetheart, we'll have our fun later," and winked at me.

Anatoly left the room as well, and I was stuck on my back lying on the wood plank. I was too weak to turn over, so I closed my eyes and slept for what could've been an hour, or eight.

I heard the door open, and some rapid Russian being spoken, then the door shut, and I heard heavy footsteps heading my way. With a solid kick, Anatoly flipped me over and pulled me up by the plank. I felt my arms stretching back too far and heard a loud pop accompanied by a brilliant flash of pain in my right shoulder. I cried out and tried to kick out at the man's knee, but he threw me against the wall and pressed against me with his full weight. He was breathing heavily in my ear and licked my neck. I screamed, but I knew no one would hear. He laughed and started struggling to pull my panties down, so I closed my eyes. *This is what they go through. All those people we've saved.* I knew it was time to dissociate so I tried not to think about what was about to happen. I heard a sudden loud bang, the familiar sound of a silenced pistol shot and felt hot blood cover my face. I opened my eyes and half of Anatoly's skull was splattered on the wall. He fell with a thud and I collapsed but was caught by a tall man with a military haircut and dark eyes. He shouted something I didn't understand as I heard bootsteps and doors kicking in throughout the suite. There was some suppressed gunfire and a quick shout, but the man was carrying me toward a different room.

"No!" I screamed, then realized he had cut the chains on my restraints. He sat me down next to the bathtub and used a wet towel to clean the blood off my face as gently as possible. More bootsteps, "What are you doing? We have to go NOW!"

"She can't get on the plane like this, for fuck's sake bring me something for her to wear."

My head was spinning as the men dressed me quickly. The smell of gasoline was overwhelming. They tried to pick me up under my arms and the pain in my shoulder caused me to vomit. The tall man scooped me up and jogged toward the door, which the other was holding open. He carried me down several flights of stairs and I started to float in and out of consciousness. I vaguely remember hearing a wailing fire alarm. I saw an alley and a van and tried to run but was caught and wrestled back into the back seat of the van filled with about seven other men. I must've lost consciousness again, because I woke up when the driver took a sharp turn and tried to kick out the window of the van but was once again subdued. "Can you sedate her, for Christ's sake?" screamed the driver. Two of the men held me down while a third injected me, and once again, I slept.

This time as I slept, I dreamt of Ravi. I heard his voice in my ear, just like the night before we went into the club. I felt his familiar hand in my own, heard him telling me I would be alright. I heard other voices, too, unfamiliar and mostly speaking Hebrew to one another softly. I thought I heard a woman speaking Hebrew as well, but with authority, and when she spoke the others listened. I tried to open my eyes but was met with a blinding light which made my head ache so I closed them and tried to sit up. "No, dear, sleep. It will stop the pain", the woman said. I felt a cool flush in my arm and slept again.

Jerusalem, Israel

"Ah, it's nice to see you waking up on your own," said the female voice from my dreams.

I was lying face down on a bed and turned painfully to look around. I was in a bedroom, that much was clear, but the rest was a mystery. The woman was older, wearing glasses and a neat bun, leaning over my back with a bright reading lamp over her shoulder. My whole body ached, and I struggled to make sense of what was going on.

She grabbed a pen light and waved it past my eyes a couple of times. "Excellent. I was afraid you may have had a brain bleed, but it looks like a simple concussion. It was hard to tell when your eyes were so swollen, but I think you'll recover from that part nicely." She returned to her work on my back.

"Where am I?" I asked.

"Jerusalem," she answered as she continued her work.

"What are you doing?"

She gave me a look that reminded me of Ravi, it was anger flashing in her eyes. "Those men that put the wood piece behind your back... it left splinters. Hundreds. But don't worry, dear, I'm almost finished now. They really did a number on you. I have no respect for men who treat women this way, it's barbaric." This woman seemed like the type of woman who's respect you would want to have.

"What... what happened? I want to know." I wasn't entirely sure I wanted to know, but I had a feeling she would tell me the truth.

"I'm not sure how this all began, if that's what you're asking.

I got a phone call from Ravi three days ago and he was frantic, insisting we all get on the plane he had chartered. So, of course, we did. When we arrived, Ravi was hysterical, planning a rescue mission for a woman, that being you, and was determined to kill the people who had done this to you." She shook her head and smiled. "Ravi can be a little dramatic. He and Hassan nearly came to blows when Hassan insisted that Ravi stay back, I've never seen them fight like that, very disturbing. The rest of the men went with Hassan while Ravi and I waited at the airport, which fortunately, was very close to the hotel where the raid was to take place."

She paused for a moment and adjusted her glasses. "He could barely function as we waited at the airport. I hadn't seen Ravi in such a state since we lost Nera." This memory seemed especially painful for her to mention, so I let her work in silence for a few moments.

"There," she said triumphantly. "This salve should soothe the abrasions," she said as she rubbed a gel across my wounds that felt glorious. Her touch was firm but had a gentleness to it It reminded me of when Ravi rubbed my back in Haiti.

She turned off the lamp, took off her glasses and rubbed the bridge of her nose. She gently helped me sit up and asked me how that felt. I nodded and told her I was ok. I tried to stretch but my right arm was wrapped tightly in a sling. I had forgotten about that part.

"You're really good at this, are you a medic?" I asked.

She looked a little surprised. "I'm actually a physician. Dr. Eleora Weiss."

Weiss??

"I'm Ravi's mother." She waited for a reaction from me, but I sat, stunned. It never occurred to me that Ravi would have a mother and that they would be close.

She laughed and began gathering her supplies. "When they brought you to the plane unconscious, the pilots refused to take off. They said it was against protocol." She rolled her eyes. "I walked into that cockpit and told them I am a physician, and this patient needs care urgently that can't be received in this country and if they didn't take off immediately, I would report them for a human rights violation." She laughed heartily, so much like Ravi. "The men had wanted to storm the cockpit and put guns to their heads but sometimes a woman's way is just better," she said, still laughing.

She put her hand on mine and looked at me seriously. "You must mean a great deal to Ravi for him to call his IDF friends *and* me to help you. And I can see from what happened to you that you're a fighter. I don't know what your relationship is to my son or what kind of business you two have gotten into, but Ravi is a good man. Losing Nera almost killed him, I don't think he could bear another loss like that." She stood up and smoothed her skirt. "I won't say another word about it, but you can get dressed if you'd like. I think there's coffee in the kitchen. Just take it easy, doctor's orders," she said with a wink.

"Wait, where do I get clothes?"

"Ravi has T-shirts and shorts in his dresser over to your left," she said.

"Is this Ravi's flat?"

"Of course, dear, where else would he take you?" She slipped out of the room quietly.

I looked around Ravi's bedroom. Comfortable king bed, modern furniture, minimalist artwork on the walls. I grabbed a T-shirt, and sweatpants which were so big for me that I had to roll the waistband down and the bottoms up. I sat on the bed to collect myself (and my energy) for a moment when I looked on his nightstand. There sat an achingly beautiful picture of Nera as a toddler next to a half-burned candle. And next to that was a photo of the travel group from Thailand. I picked it up and looked closer, we had all spent the day at the beach and were a little tipsy when Diana wanted to get a group photo. We all stood and smiled then she wanted a silly shot, so Ravi scooped me up like a bride and I wrapped my arms around his neck, laughing. I remembered this day so well because I had the same picture on my desk in my study.

I walked slowly, and painfully, down the short hall and around a corner to see a spacious living room, open to the kitchen and dining area with dark wood floors. In the living area was a huge sectional sofa, upon which two men (I'm guessing part of the team) were watching the news. Dr. Weiss sat on the other corner flipping through a magazine, two more men sat at the dining room table playing chess and another was in the kitchen washing dishes and cleaning up after what smelled like a delicious dinner. It appeared to be late evening, but I really had no sense of time or how long I had been there. I realized that everyone stopped what they were doing and stared at me.

"Um… could I have some coffee, please?" I asked no one in particular.

The man in the kitchen swiftly went to the cabinet for a mug. I looked at the enormous TV and saw that there had been a fire at the penthouse of the Palazzo Versace in Dubai, and foul play was suspected. I wondered if that's where I had been taken. I jumped when the man touched my shoulder to hand me my coffee. "Thank you," I whispered. He just nodded and went back into the kitchen. I leaned over Dr. Weiss, "Where's Ravi?"

"He's finally sleeping, you should let him get some rest. He has been through a lot in the last couple days", she nodded toward the tall glass doors behind the table. "Hassan is on the balcony; he may be able to answer some questions for you."

Hassan, I thought fuzzily. *Hassan was his partner in IDF.*

I walked gingerly over to the sliding doors and stepped outside. It was a warm evening, and the balcony had a dazzling view of the Jerusalem skyline. I took a moment to feel the breeze, touched with the scent of wisteria and incense, and admire the skyline when I heard a gravelly voice say, "Glad to see you're conscious." I looked to the corner of the balcony and saw Hassan, dressed in a fitted tank top and basketball shorts. He was much more muscular than I remember, huge, really. He took a drink of his beer and lit a cigarette. I tried not to look intimidated.

"Thank you for rescuing me," I said directly.

"It was hardly a rescue, you fought me every step of the way. Did you think I was kidnapping you?"

"Well... yes."

He regarded me for a moment and we both laughed. I slowly sat in the opposite chair and gazed out at the view.

"What exactly happened?" I asked. I didn't know if I wanted the answer, but my curiosity always wins.

Hassan took a long drag and spoke with smoke coming out of his mouth. "Ravi called me saying he needed me for a mission. I didn't even question it, Ravi and I," he thumped his chest with his fist, "like brothers. I got on the plane. He briefed me on the mission, but he was in no shape to participate, he was a mess. I hadn't seen him like that since we lost Nera."

We, I thought. They really are family.

"I insisted I lead the mission and he stay behind. For the first time in our lives, he tried to attack me. The men held him back, he was swinging on me like he actually wanted to fight me. This wasn't normal. So, I assured him I would handle it. I think I may be the only person in the world that he would have allowed to lead that mission." He took a long drink and a long drag. The man was in no rush, but the suspense was killing me. "I think they had you there maybe 24 hours total. We took the stairwell to the penthouse, broke down the door, and you remember the rest, right?"

"A little. Some of the details are hazy. I remember smelling gasoline. And you carrying me down some stairs."

He laughed. "Some stairs? Try eleven stories! Good thing you're as light as you are, I'm not as strong as I used to be! We had to burn the evidence; they'll never know it was us. Unless…" he stopped himself abruptly and glanced at me quickly. "Anyway, we boarded the plane which was only a couple miles from the hotel and Ma got us in the air."

I thought about this. Something is missing. Yes, they rescued me, but what did he mean by "unless"? I reached for my locket and realized it was missing then it clicked for me. "The Russian."

Hassan furrowed his brow. "Gregori Vasiliev, oil tycoon, made some shady deals with some people to build his fortune, using slave labor from Madagascar, things like that. And he's certifiably insane. Has some unique perversions, so he travels a lot to keep from getting caught. Ravi has been trying to track him for the last two days nonstop but hasn't had any luck."

"He… he got away?" my heart began to race.

"Down the penthouse elevator and out the front fucking door while we were upstairs. If we'd had more men it would've been a more secure mission, but…" he trailed off with a waving of his hand.

I took a few deep breaths trying to calm myself. I didn't know how much information he could find on me, or the kids for that matter. I didn't even know if I really registered on his radar as someone important enough to look for. But, with his paranoid delusions he may lock on to me as an obsession. There's really no telling which way this could go, but I knew I had to be very careful.

"He'll find him, you know. Ravi is very good at this," Hassan tried to reassure me. He leaned forward with his elbows on his knees. "Especially if it's someone important he is trying to protect." He raised an eyebrow at me but did not smile. I looked away.

We sat in silence for a few moments, me drinking my coffee, he his beer. He stood up and started to walk towards the door, but stopped. "You may not know this, but you are important to him. I saw it without him saying a word. So, if whatever you two are into gets my brother killed, I'll kill you." I looked at him with wide eyes, that was a pretty intense threat from such an imposing man. "Also, you aren't allowed to die. Ever." He smiled and patted me gently on my good shoulder as he walked inside.

11

Looking out at the skyline at the sunset, I tried to clear my mind and not think about the mentally unstable Russian who might be looking for me. I thought about Jenna and Ethan, the ocean, going back to sleep in Ravi's big comfortable bed. I forced myself to think about anything peaceful to try to ease my raging anxiety. I finished my coffee and opened the big door to enter the flat and found that everyone had left except Dr. Weiss. She was putting her things in her big Gucci bag and looked up at me.

"Emelia, I must go. It's getting late. I left some of that salve and some pain meds for you in the kitchen. Don't go easy on the pain meds, you don't need to be a martyr and you'll be in quite a lot of pain for a few days," she said as she gave me a serious look. To my surprise, she embraced me, smelling of a luxurious but unfamiliar perfume, and said, "Take care of yourself. Have Ravi call me when he wakes." And she was out the door, and I was alone. In Ravi's flat.

I took this chance to really get a look around. It was clean, and bachelor tidy with a few magazines and some mail on the coffee table but nothing else really out of place. There was a modern wooden bench by the entryway, and he had all his boots lined up under it. *Why just the boots?* I wondered but I kept investigating. He had simple and tasteful artwork on all the walls except for the wall that contained a huge built-in bookcase. I looked through the titles, mostly Hebrew and unrecognizable to me. I did recognize something, my two books on the very top shelf. I smiled at this. Beneath the TV sat an electronics case with all the latest gadgets, of course. And leaning against the electronics case was an acoustic guitar.

Ravi plays the guitar?

I wandered into the modern kitchen with sleek black cabinetry and ultra-modern light fixtures. He had a designer Swedish knife set on the counter along with a full spice rack, which told me he cooks. I couldn't remember if I knew this about him or if he ever mentioned it. He had a stocked pantry and a refrigerator with all the essentials, some fresh grapes and strawberries, and a few bottles of beer. It felt so weird, looking into the life Ravi lived outside our missions, I wondered who he was in this different life and suddenly I felt like I didn't belong here.

I went into the master bathroom, turned on the light and gasped at my reflection in the huge mirror. I had two black and swollen eyes with a huge knot in between. Someone, I'm guessing Dr. Weiss, had cleanly sutured a wound there but I don't know if my nose had been broken or if I would be left with a scar. I carefully slipped out of Ravi's clothes and shuddered when I realized I was still wearing the same black panties from the hotel room. I took them off quickly and threw them away. I looked in the mirror again, my body was covered in bruises and abrasions, and when I took off the sling, I saw my entire shoulder was bruised and it still hurt to lift my arm. When I saw my lower back, I realized what Dr. Weiss meant. There were hundreds of abrasions, it must've taken her hours to take out all those splinters. I looked wrecked, and I felt it, too.

I turned on the shower, which was a fabulous waterfall shower, and took a long, hot, glorious shower. Of course, Ravi had women's soap in his shower, so I washed my entire body three times and stepped out feeling better, but exhausted. I toweled off, ran my fingers through my hair, and found a spare toothbrush in the cabinet. I went into the kitchen to take some of the pain meds Dr. Weiss had left for me, which were powerful enough to lull me into a deep sleep, wrapped in Ravi's thick duvet.

Ravi's bedroom had an eastern window with beautiful light in the morning. I laid in bed and enjoyed it for a while, until I felt the need for some more pain meds. Despite Dr. Weiss's admonition, I didn't want to take too much. I needed to be mentally aware, just in case. I stood up and stretched the stiffness out of my still sore body and tried to move my arm around a little to loosen up my shoulder. It hurt, but my mobility was better. I was healing. The flat was quiet, so I suspected Ravi was still asleep and I went straight to the kitchen to try to figure out his high-tech coffee maker. I heard a door close and Ravi walked out of the hall, shirtless, looking at some satellite photos and whistling to himself. He looked up at me and dropped the photos, standing perfectly still for what felt like minutes. A look of horror had come over his face, I assumed because I looked so terrible in that moment.

"Good morning," I said. He said nothing. "It'll heal, I'm ok, I know I look really bad now…" I began but he swiftly crossed the room and gently caressed my broken face.

"No, Mia, you're beautiful. And alive." He wrapped his arms around me and held me to his chest. "You're alive," he repeated as if he couldn't believe it without seeing me and talking to me. He looked at my face again, looking sad. "Want coffee?" he asked brightly.

I smiled, "God, yes."

We drank coffee on the balcony, watching the busy streets. "So, I met your mother. She's nice," I said. We both laughed at the bizarre circumstances of the meeting.

"She's a strong woman, raised me on her own after my father died when I was only two. She always worked hard, very passionate about what she does. She's head of cardiothoracic surgery now at the Hadassah Medical Center, worked her way up. She's... pushy," he said with a good-natured eye roll. I imagined her, a young widow, working long hours as a surgeon while raising a two-year-old all alone. No wonder she is so tough.

"Also, you play the guitar?" I asked skeptically.

"I wouldn't say that, I learned to play exactly two songs, which is all you need to get women to sleep with you," he said mischievously. I gave him a playful slap on the arm, and he responded, "I could play for you if you'd like but I don't think you're in any condition to fall into bed with me and I know you wouldn't be able to resist." I was laughing hard, which hurt my bruised ribs, but I didn't care, it felt so good to laugh.

We sat on the balcony for hours, he brought out my wholewheat toast and more coffee and told me about every man on the team. They all had such a history; it was no wonder they behaved like family. Especially Hassan, Ravi told me all about how their relationship evolved over time. Hassan had been married with four children and his wife left him to move to Europe with another man, and it was Ravi who consoled him when he cried, then hit every bar in Israel when he wanted to drink, then fought alongside him when Hassan inevitably picked a fight at these bars. It was a dark time in Hassan's life and Ravi was with him in the darkness every step of the way. He said Hassan has moved on, doesn't quite drink like he used to, "Which is very fortunate for me, because I don't think I could keep up with him anymore," Ravi said laughing. Instead, they developed the kind of relationship that just exists as it is, through pain and

119

happiness, they are a constant for each other.

We went into the kitchen to rinse our dishes from breakfast when there was a knock at the door. I ducked behind the counter, reaching for my pistol (which wasn't there) but my arm was pinned down by the sling and causing a shooting pain through my arm into my shoulder, while Ravi casually walked to the door.

"Ravi, no!" I yelled from my hiding place, but he gave me a confused look and opened the door.

No gunshots, no Russian coming to kidnap me, just a brief exchange with another man in Hebrew and Ravi shut the door. "Mia, it's just a package my mother sent for you, what are you doing?" He looked at me quizzically. I walked over to the couch, shaking, my heart racing.

"You shouldn't have opened that door! It could've been anyone! Don't you realize how much danger I'm in?" I shouted.

"Mia, Mia, you aren't in danger right now..."

"Yes, I am!" I looked around frantically to try to gather my things, but I had nothing there. "I need to leave right now, I need to be somewhere safe."

"You *are* safe. You are safe here," he said as he enveloped me in a tight hug. In his arms, all my fear rushed out, it was an enormous release and I burst into tears. He held me and stroked my hair while I cried harder than I ever had in my life. He sat me on the couch and continued to hold me while I cried. Gradually, I began to relax, and the tears slowed to a trickle but didn't stop entirely. I told him about the hotel room and how it felt when I was certain I was about to be raped. "These women, the children, for God's sake, how do they endure this every day?" and I unleashed a new freshet of tears.

Ravi sat up, he said, "Do you want to know what happened with the children we rescued that day? The day you were taken.

I thought about it for a moment. "Yes, I do."

He told me that although he had concerns about leaving, he trusted that I would find my way to the rendezvous point like I always do. He drove the truck as far as the road would take him, then started walking the children across the mile-long stretch to the main road. Though they hadn't slept much and were probably exhausted, the hike must have felt amazing for them. It was freedom, it was being outside. They raced each other, even in the heat, and laughed. Toward the end Ravi and the older children had to carry some of the smaller ones, but they finally reached the buses from OUR. The group had brought cold water and food for the children, so they all had a picnic in the bus while Ravi waited for me to show up. After half an hour, he started to worry. Then, one of the children was given a soccer ball and he saw a dozen of these rescued children playing a regular soccer game, just like regular children should be doing. It was *the* moment for Ravi that told him what we were doing was worth all the effort we had put into it. An hour after their arrival, he told OUR to take the children and he would contact them if there were more. He needed to get back and find me. So, he jogged back to the truck and went back to the nightclub.

"Emelia, I don't think you are ready to hear the next part, so we can discuss it another time. I just wanted you to know that the children were safe. Not just safe, but they were playing. There is a life out there for them and they were already starting to live it. They won't be suffering anymore because of what we do." This was a powerful statement. It was exactly what I needed to hear. I dried my tears, sighed and laid down, being careful not to lay on my right side and tucked my knees into my chest. Ravi slid in behind me carefully and wrapped his arms around me, holding me until I fell asleep.

We decided at the insistence of Dr. Weiss (who also insisted I call her Eleora) that I should stay in Israel another week. "Your children shouldn't see you looking like this. You need to heal," she said authoritatively. I knew I had a difficult call to make to Bryce, but as I picked up Ravi's phone, I decided to call Laura instead. She may be more... understanding.

"Hello?" she said.

"Hey, Laura, it's Emelia. I had a little trouble in Dubai, and I'll be staying here a week longer than expected."

"Oh no, are you ok?" She sounded worried.

"Of course, just a parasailing accident. Dislocated my shoulder, broke my nose, it was a little ugly. But I'm fine. Do you mind keeping the kids longer? And letting them know I'm ok?"

"No problem, that sounds terrifying. I'm glad you're ok, though," she said.

"Yes, on the mend. Give the children my love, I'll pick them up in a week."

"Of course, take care Emilia." She hung up.

"That was easy," Ravi said walking through the living room to his office. He spent hours in there, working on his massive computer setup that I couldn't even begin to understand. I think he was still looking for Gregori, but he never mentioned it to me.

The rest of the week was a time for healing, but less for the physical injuries and more for the emotional injuries. It turns out the package from Eleora was a box of designer loungewear, panties, bras, and basically anything a woman would need to get through a week. She even sent a note, "Take care of yourself, xx, Eleora". I spent most of my time reading the few English books Ravi had and watching reruns of Friends, which Ravi had generously equipped with English subtitles. I did have moments where I would break down crying for no reason and Ravi would always wrap me in a tight hug and hold me until it passed. The first night I fell asleep in his room I asked him to put a pistol on the nightstand for me, for peace of mind. He hesitated, then said, "As long as you promise not to shoot me in the middle of the night" with a very serious look. I threw a pillow at him and laughed, and he went to get the pistol shouting, "You are so aggressive, I think you just might shoot me after all!" He laid it on the nightstand and left the door open in case I got scared in the middle of the night. I knew I could find him in the guest bedroom, but I wanted to sleep alone.

I did learn a lot about Ravi during that week. I was right about the cooking, he loved to cook always turning up Rolling Stones, Coldplay, The Beatles, Soundgarden, depending on his mood and he would sing along as he cooked. He made it look fun, and I have to admit, sexy. And the food was terrific, he really knew how to take a simple dish and make it into something savory and exotic. He read the paper cover to cover every morning because, "he likes to feel the pages in his hands" instead of reading online. And he loved fresh flowers, going out every morning for the day's groceries and coming in with a different bouquet every day that he would arrange in a vase on the dining room table. We coexisted peacefully, I didn't want to interrupt his work and he wanted to give me whatever space I needed but it was a comfortable coexistence. I was comforted just by the fact that he was there.

The last night I was there he insisted on getting me out of the house. We left in the early evening and walked a short distance to a lovely open-air café. They served traditional Israeli cuisine and I was shocked to find how much I loved the tabbouleh and was surprised at how much I liked the sambusak, which I only tried at Ravi's insistence. We drank wine with our meal and laughed as we reminisced about some of our more interesting vacations. It occurred to me as he picked up the check, that this would be considered a date, if we were two normal people.

On the walk home Ravi grabbed my hand, "I'm proud of you for today. I knew you were nervous leaving the house, but you did terrific." He looked at me with his big brown eyes and I just squeezed his hand and held it the rest of the way to the flat. I had been nervous, but I think he just took me out to calm my nerves before I had to go to the airport tomorrow. Not a date, a mission. Perhaps.

At the airport, Ravi carried a small bag he had given me for the things I had gotten from Eleora. We waited briefly at the terminal, then the boarding call came.

"Ravi."

"Emelia."

But, instead of a handshake he took a couple steps closer, he was leaning close to my face. He grabbed my hands in his, then hesitated. I thought he was going to kiss me and my heart started pounding. He gave me a gentle kiss on the cheek and said, "Until next time." He turned and walked away while I stood, heart still racing. After a few moments, I finally turned to go board my flight.

12
2019
Hanover, New Hampshire

Picking up the kids went fairly smoothly. Bryce wished me well, but Laura eyed me suspiciously with the sling and the bruises still on my face. The kids were an easier sell, I made up an exciting story about parasailing and crashing on a rock, wanting to sue the company, and recovering in a hospital.

"Mom, you really should be more careful. You could've been killed!" Ethan said, concernedly.

No kidding, I thought. "No, these kinds of accidents are very rare. But I don't think I'll go parasailing again," I said with a laugh. Jenna laughed, too, and all seemed fine.

The first thing I did when I got home was have a high-tech security system installed with motion activated cameras and all the bells and whistles. I'm sure Ravi wouldn't approve, since he could hack something like that, but I reminded myself not everyone was a world-class hacker and felt a little safer. I wasn't sleeping well, waking with nightmares frequently, so I was waking up earlier for my runs and making sure I carried my pistol everywhere. The following Monday I was back at work and grateful for the distraction.

Toward the end of that week, I got a call from Laura in the middle of the morning.

"Hello?" This was unusual.

"Emelia, hey, could you meet me for coffee during your lunch break? We need to talk." She sounded serious; this couldn't be good.

"I don't know, I'm pretty busy with…"

"Please," she interrupted. "It's really important." I sighed.

"Sure, let's do it." I hated having unexpected things like this happen.

We met at a Starbucks close to campus. Baby TJ was with his grandmother, apparently this conversation needed her full attention. We ordered our drinks and sat down. She looked at me for a few moments, then folded her hand around her coffee cup.

"You called me from an Israeli number last week. Were you in Israel when you called?" Damn, straight to the point.

"Yes."

She paused. "I asked Jenna casually if anyone in your group was from Israel. She said this guy Ravi was, and you and he trade emails about the vacation destination a lot. Then Ethan told me that you've been having nightmares where you wake up screaming and he caught you checking the house for intruders with a gun!"

"Yes." I crossed my arms, not sure where this was going, but unwilling to give any unnecessary details.

Laura sighed and surprised me by putting her hands face down on the table, manicure sparkling, and leaning forward angrily. "Are you in an abusive relationship with this Ravi guy?"

That shocked me, totally catching me off guard. "Umm…no, uh, no, Ravi and I are not in a relationship!" I stammered.

"Ok, fine, call it what you want, but is he abusing you? Because I can't stand for a woman to stay in an abusive… anything." She was definitely angry, but not at me.

"No, Laura, I'm not being abused."

She grabbed both of my hands in hers, "Look, if you are, we don't have to talk about it. You and the kids can just move in with me and Bryce until you figure something out. You have options here. I can talk Bryce into it, don't worry about that, I just want to make sure you're safe." She was genuinely concerned; I was actually touched. But something struck me as strange about what she just said.

"Wait, you haven't talked to Bryce about this have you?" I asked.

She looked away, guiltily.

"Why not?" I pressed, gently.

She shook her head and shrugged. "Some things just need to stay between women." I knew she had a close group of women friends, but I thought it was shallow socializing. But to offer your husband's ex-wife to move in with you is not shallow. She's a *woman's* woman, something that came as a big surprise to me.

"Laura, do you know what I do for a living?" I asked.

"Well, you teach, and you write books, right"

"Do you know what I specialize in?" I asked.

"Sex trafficking," she leaned in a little closer as she said this.

"Can you keep a secret?" I asked. She nodded slowly and took a deep breath. I told her about the missions Ravi and I did. I told her we went to different countries to save the women and children and link them up with groups that could help them. I spared her the details about the killing (making her complicit in dozens, maybe hundreds of murders may not be a good gesture) but I told her sometimes it got dangerous.

She leaned back in her seat and crossed her arms. I waited a full two minutes for her to speak, terrified that she wouldn't believe me or that she would turn me in. Finally, she said, "It's about damn time somebody did something about it." She smiled widely.

"You're kind of a badass, aren't you?" she said with a grin

as we gathered our stuff to leave.

"No, I'm not a badass. But it is pretty exciting sometimes," I said hoping to downplay the danger of it.

"Just promise me you'll be careful, for the kids' sake. I won't tell a soul." I could see she really meant that.

"I promise." And that's how Laura and I started having coffee together once a week with Bryce being none the wiser.

Three weeks later I was at home researching the next location, still unsure if I was willing to leave the relative safety of my home, when I got a small package in the mail. There was no return address. I opened it carefully and inside was a small wooden box. Hesitantly, I opened that, and there sat my grandmother's locket, with both pictures still inside and a new solid gold chain. My heart was racing but I reached for the note inside and read:

You are safe.

I gasped and sprinted to my computer. I googled "Gregori Vasiliev" and a news article popped up saying he was found dead on his yacht of an apparent suicide off the coast of Greece. I picked up my phone, hesitated, then texted Ravi:

Have you been vacationing without me?

Moments later he replied with a winky kiss face. I smiled and shook my head. I pulled the locket out and put it around my neck and felt my anxiety start to slip away. I sat down at the computer and started researching the Philippines with a little more gusto.

13
October 2019
Washington, D.C.

When I went back to work, I was approached by a Senator about doing some research into prostitution and human trafficking victims in the United States who were prosecuted for prostitution. She wanted to introduce a bill that reduced prosecution and provided more rehabilitation and opportunities for the men and women affected by this.

"You seem to be the expert in the field, your books were very inspiring," she told me during our first phone conference.

"Thank you, I feel very passionately about this issue. I think we can come up with something really good here and change some lives," I told her.

I dove into the research and provided all the statistics and data she would need to support the bill on the Senate floor. Throughout my research, I found myself linked up with a member of USAID, who could be critical in the implementation of the bill. Catherine Crawford would call me a dozen times a day as we were perfecting our research, so naturally, we became close.

"You know what would help?" she said thoughtfully over a lunch meeting. "A gala. Something big to get support from other politicians, they love that stuff. And we could get a lot more donors to support this." Catherine *would* love something like that, she had flawless dark skin, natural hair, and always looked glamorous, even in casual clothes and no makeup (because she didn't need it).

On the other hand, I hated all the begging and sucking up involved in these events, but she was right. Politicians loved having people throw a big affair to get their support. "Yes, I think you're right. Do I have to go?" We laughed as we finished our lunch.

The next day I was complaining to Laura about how much I loathed these events and she perked up. "You know I used to be an event planner in New York?" *What?* I had a hard time imagining Laura as a working girl instead of a mama in yoga pants. And planning events in New York usually meant swanky parties and expensive weddings so if that's the case, she could handle the amount of glamor we needed for this event.

"You did?"

She nodded and told me, "Girl, I got this. I still have my contacts for D.C. if you want me to plan it." There was a hopeful tone to her voice, I think she was itching to get her hands on some work, even if it was just a one-time thing.

"I'll have to run it by Catherine to get the funding, but between you and me, you're hired" I said, and we shook hands with her smiling triumphantly.

Laura turned out to be a terrific planner, she communicated with Catherine about all the details (because I didn't want anything to do with that part of it) and Catherine gushed about Laura's design aesthetic and her networking skills. It was two days before the event, my speech was written so all I had to do was find the perfect dress. Of course, this was a job for Laura. I picked her up at her house, with Bryce standing at the door looking at us skeptically.

"Laura, how does Bryce feel about us working together?" I asked as we turned toward the boutique she suggested.

"He doesn't feel anything, I guess, he just always looks at me baffled when I talk about it," she giggled a little at this.

"Well, you know, you're supposed to hate the ex-wife and I'm supposed to be bitter about the new wife," I joked. We both laughed at this.

The boutique looked upscale, and I was immediately intimidated. Laura picked up on that, "Don't worry, I called ahead and told them we would need someone's full attention." Laura always had things like this covered.

We walked in and there were a few gowns on display, some luxurious furniture in a sitting area, and a marble counter behind which stood a tall, willowy girl who introduced herself as Henna. Laura did all the talking, telling Henna about the event, the style she thought would look best on me, and even specified the fabric type the dress needed to be. When Laura was working, she was all business, even a little bitchy, but she got results. Henna rushed to the store-room to find something to match Laura's specifications. She brought out a few dresses which Laura immediately dismissed and sent her back with more specific instructions delivered more firmly. Henna dashed to the back and Laura gave me a sweet smile. I giggled; she could be such a contradiction. Finally, Henna produced a simple, blue strapless dress with a thigh slit. I looked at it uncertainly, a thigh slit? Laura whispered, "Trust me" and shoved me into the dressing room. I put it on and looked in the mirror and was shocked. It made my shoulders look terrific and the thigh slit wasn't terribly high but made me look three inches taller.

I spun around and walked a little to make sure it was comfortable and Henna chimed in, "That color makes your eyes look amazing!" This was definitely *the* gown.

The night of the event I wore my hair in a simple updo with

subtle jewelry. I didn't want to distract from my speech. The event was at The National Portrait Gallery and it was beautiful, professional, and worth every penny we spent on Laura's expertise. Laura kept it subtle and elegant, there was a stage with a podium off to the side and a huge white screen behind it for presentations. It had the same gold swag that hung from the tables and chairs, and the event was mostly candlelit. It was also packed with politicians; you could hardly grab a drink without running into someone powerful. I was about to go onstage, and Laura was touching up my makeup and hyping me up.

"What do you think of the speech?" I asked her. I knew she would tell me the truth.

"Honestly, I think it's a little bland, but appropriate for the audience. Ok, you're up, knock 'em dead!" She ushered me toward the stage. I walked to the podium and began my bland speech with a matching PowerPoint presentation to represent the data visually. I could see the guests getting antsy, they were starting to talk among themselves and get up to go get drinks. I paused and looked at the data on the screen for a moment.

"This... this is a lot of data. I'm a research scientist so this is what I do, I take data and extract meaning from it. But this part is not the meaning, I mean, how many of you really care about which statistical formula we used to reach our conclusion?" I asked, raising my hand. The audience laughed a little. "Yeah, that isn't the true meaning of this data. We aren't here for numbers; we are here for the people. What do you think of when you think of a prostitute? Poor, maybe a minority, turning tricks to support a drug habit? Sometimes that's true, but did you know that 90% of prostitutes work for a pimp? That means 90% of prostitutes are being bought and sold for someone else's benefit, they are nothing more than a product, a commodity. *That's* the problem, selling humans."

"Worldwide, there are forty-two million prostitutes. Just thinking of that number is meaningless. But, if you consider that each one of those forty-two million is a human being with a soul, a family, emotions, responsibilities, thoughts and feelings, the number seems much bigger. More meaningful. And, it makes us more inclined to want to restore these human beings' dignity by providing resources for rehabilitation, not punishment. I guarantee, the prostitute who is bailed out of jail by her pimp isn't going home to a massage and a glass of wine. He'll probably beat her and will likely kill her." The audience was starting to really pay attention now.

"We have to decide what we want. Do we want justice?" I thought about the justice Ravi and I delivered. "Go after the traffickers and the customers and give them the harsher punishments they deserve. Do we want to make the world a better place? In that case, we have to help the *victims* instead of prosecuting them. We all are responsible to each other and to humanity as a whole, helping the most vulnerable and exploited is not just an obligation. It's a moral imperative." The audience seemed to love my veering off script and gave me a very generous standing ovation. I could feel every eye on me as I walked across the stage. Catherine was on next and met me in the middle of the stage and embraced me fully, "You did great, sis!" she told me before walking to the podium.

"Emelia!" I heard a familiar and exuberant voice. I looked around and saw none other than Mark and Julia from our travel group. I was surprised to see them here and hugged them as we exchanged pleasantries. "Fantastic speech, well done! Isn't this event just lovely? Have you met our son, William?"

A nice-looking blond man in a tuxedo grabbed my hand,

"It's a pleasure to meet you, mum and dad have told me all about you," he smiled.

We sat at a table together to catch up, and when William left to get drinks, Julia hinted, "He's divorced. Just so you know," and winked at me. *Bold move, Julia*, I thought, but I just smiled. He returned and gave us all drinks, smiling broadly at me. I took a long drink and checked my watch.

My research on the Philippines was proving to be way more complex and difficult than any other location we had researched. Manilla was hot, too hot, and full of rivalling gangs so the opportunities there, though there were many, were too much for a two-person team. The surrounding islands had a thriving sex tourism industry, but it was widespread with numerous leaders and pimps and they rarely brought in large transports of people, it was one or two at a time to sidestep the new regulations that had been put in place to minimize sex trafficking. The regulations were a step in the right direction, but it simply wasn't enough to stop it. Ravi was having some trouble, as well. He found plenty of places and plenty of powerful warlords but nothing that was within our scope. We would need to come up with an idea fast and on the fly, because tourist week was next week, and we still hadn't nailed down a solid plan.

I sat back in my desk chair in my study and tried to think. I looked at the photo from Thailand. We extended that trip and hit several places to get the numbers we wanted, and it was one of our most successful missions. But it was all in one place, the Philippines consist of 7,641 islands, there was no way we could approach this with our usual style and have any level of success. Max jumped into my lap purring, reminding me gently that it was time for bed. I wanted to spend some time with the kids this week, so I took some extra time off work, I needed to get to bed early to take them out to the lake the next day. I reluctantly shut down my computer and went to bed, trying to think outside the box for another hour before falling asleep.

December 2019

Hanover, New Hampshire

I pulled into Bryce and Laura's driveway, hoping nothing would be unusual about this drop off. I knew it had been risky telling Laura about what I do on my "vacations", but I usually have good instincts about who can be trusted. Turns out I was right, Laura could keep a secret because Bryce didn't say anything to stop me or act overly concerned and the kids didn't give me an extended or dramatic goodbye, just the usual hugs and cheerful, "Bye, Mom! Love you!" Laura did come give me a big hug and whispered, "Go get 'em". Then as she was walking back to the house she said over her shoulder, "No more parasailing!" and we all laughed. I drove to the airport still racking my brain about the plan, desperate to give Ravi at least something to work with at our briefing.

Manila, Philippines

I waited nervously for Ravi, scrounging photos, articles, maps, books, and anything else I could find that may give me something to hit on. I was so engrossed in a map that I didn't realize he was there until I heard his familiar, "Emelia".

I looked up at him and at once felt calmer, he was smirking at me and looked totally relaxed. "Ravi," I said with relief. He started pulling out his notes and photos and we immediately began comparing what we had, which didn't amount to much. "I keep coming back to Mindoro Island, it's *the* hotspot but I'm not sure how we can make this happen logistically," I told him, showing him the map and a fact sheet about the island.

"You know, at some point, I think we'll need to do some kind of boat transport for an island country. This could get tricky with law enforcement," he mentioned.

"Don't worry too much about that as far as transport goes, I'm working with USAID on this one."

His eyebrows shot up. "A government agency? You know they'll be tight with local law enforcement and they may not like our... techniques."

"Oh, we'll be long gone by then, of that I'm certain. Don't worry so much," I said with a grin.

"Ha! Coming from the Queen of Anxiety!" we laughed.

We sat in silence for a moment, then I decided to just say it. "Thank you for getting my locket back. You have no idea what that meant for me." I blushed and couldn't make eye contact.

"I know exactly what it meant for you, that's why I did it," he looked directly at me, making me blush deeper.

I stood up, "Let's go find the group," and started packing up my documents. He chuckled to himself and followed suit. We walked in comfortable silence to the terminal to meet up with our travel group for what would end up being our last vacation all together.

14

Dinner was at the resort's swanky restaurant, so we all dressed to the nines to make a real experience out of it. As we reached the table Julia subtly shuffled the seating arrangement, so William and I were sitting next to each other. Ravi sat directly across from me. Mark introduced William to the group and when he got to me, William interrupted, "Oh, we've already met. You are impossible to forget," and he actually kissed my hand. From the corner of my eye, I saw Ravi roll his eyes and take a long drink. We all discussed life and work, but everyone was curious about William, and he was very garrulous, telling us about his life and work in London. He mentioned that he worked for a major publishing house in London and said, "Emelia, you've published, right?" I told him who I had worked with. "Well, here's my card. If you are ever interested in switching, I would adore working with you," eliciting another dramatic eye roll from Ravi. Diana asked Ravi how his work was going, and he replied, "Oh, you know, just top-secret Israeli government tech production. Not much to talk about," and smirked at William. After dinner, we all went our separate ways, with some of us going to the main resort and others to the beachside villas. I splurged on this trip to book a beachside villa because the resort boasted open bedrooms with long canvas curtains so you could sleep listening to the sound of the ocean, which sounded marvelous to me.

Ravi caught up with me to walk me to my villa, a quarter mile down the beach. "So… how did you meet William?" He said "William" with a sneer.

"We met at a human rights gala in DC, Mark and Julia had brought him and introduced us."

"A human rights gala," Ravi scoffed. "Seems like a sleazy way to get into a girl's pants to me."

"He is NOT trying to get into my pants," I insisted. I didn't like where this conversation was going.

"Ha! He kissed your hand! Come on, I know you aren't that naïve," he grumbled. "And he certainly likes to talk about himself."

He did actually talk about himself a lot, but to be fair, the group was asking a lot of questions. "Well, I thought he seemed nice."

"Nice? That guy? Yeah, nice and boring, if you ask me," he shoved his hands in his pockets as we reached the villa.

"Tomorrow morning for a run?" he asked, but he seemed distracted.

"Only if you want to get your ass smoked by a woman again," I joked.

He laughed a big Ravi laugh and said, "Keep dreaming, short stuff!" and jogged off to his room.

The next evening the Saito's, the Japanese couple, said they wanted to visit a certain dance club on one of the islands. They usually just passively went where the group went, so we all wanted to join them. And we were all terribly curious: what kind of dance club would attract a late middle-aged couple? I dressed in my favorite wrap skirt, tank top, wedge heels and added a few bangles at the last minute. I wasn't sure how to dress for a dance club, but at least I felt comfortable. We took a slow easy pontoon ride to a small island and it felt like we walked into 1945.

The dance club was one of those local treasures you have to know about to find, and the Saito's knew. It was designed to look like a bar from the 1940's and played American swing and jazz from the '40s and '50s. It was by far the coolest place we had been as a group so far. We found a table large enough to accommodate the group and ordered a round of drinks. A real jazzy tune came on and the Saito's took to the floor. They knew the steps and the right moves for swing dancing, they skipped the really acrobatic stuff, but seeing him twirl her around made them look twenty years younger and very much in love. We all applauded their dancing, amazed that they could move like that. Ravi cozied up to a blond at the bar, but watched the couple as well, cheering them on.

William chatted me up, ordering a couple more rounds while almost everyone in the group tried their best to swing dance. It was great fun, there was a lot of laughing, stepping on toes, and valiant efforts at genuine swing dancing. Ravi sauntered over to the table and took his seat. "Can you believe those two? Now, that's real dancing, nobody does that anymore."

William stood up and took off his jacket, "I don't know, I may have a few tricks up my sleeve. Emelia?" He held his hand out to me.

Ravi scoffed, "Emelia doesn't dance." I raised my eyebrows at him, finished my drink, and stood up, smoothing my skirt.

"I took two semesters of swing dancing as an undergrad for P.E. credit. I may still have a little something." Ravi clenched his jaw and watched as William led me to the dance floor.

I admit, I was a little rusty at first, but William knew his stuff and helped me remember. We started with a simple jitterbug with a few twirls and turns just to shake the dust off. Then, "In the Mood", the perfect swing song came on and William said, "Time to shine, yeah?" I nodded and smiled, and we began a more complicated six step Lindy Hop. This dance has lots of kicks and spins and bounce to it, I was having a blast. We spun and turned then he squeezed my right hand giving me the signal to slide under his legs and we executed the move perfectly and the whole table cheered. Our big finish was one where he picked me up and spun me around, landing on his hip while he dipped me back and I kicked a leg up to make it more dramatic. Our group rose to their feet cheering, while I heard the smooth trumpet intro of one of my favorite Billie Holliday songs, Night and Day. William turned me around for another dance, but my hand was snatched from his and Ravi pulled me to the middle of the dance floor, then gently held my left hand and placed his left hand on my lower back.

"That's no way to ask a lady to dance," I said jokingly.

"Shut up," he replied with a grin and we began to sway slowly to the rhythm. It should've been no surprise to me that Ravi and I would dance well together, we knew each other's movements from our missions, so this was like that... but different.

Whether near me or far, it's no matter where you are, I think of you night and day...

He pulled me closer to him gently, resting our hands on his chest while our bodies were pressed against each other, swaying in perfect time. I wrapped my arm around his neck and laid my head on his chest, closing my eyes. Smelling his familiar Ravi scent.

There's an, oh, such a hungry yearning burning inside of me...

The music was hypnotic, and I listened to Ravi's heart beating slowly, his arm wrapped around my waist, so we were almost in a full embrace, just swaying. Feeling the warmth of each other's body close.

The song came to a close, and another livelier song began, but we stayed like that together for just a moment longer. I heard his heart begin to speed up and he lifted his hands and ran them through my hair and held my face close to his, his lips softly parted. Then he turned abruptly, and walked back to the bar, taking his seat next to the blond and ordering them another round.

Flustered, I took my seat at our table. No one said a word, apparently the group was just as shocked by that as I was. I glanced over and saw Ravi leaving the bar with the pretty blond. William ordered me another drink and tried to engage me in some more conversation, but I was too distracted to be good company. Halfway through my drink, I excused myself and left the club. I walked toward the pier to meet the ferry that would take me back to the resort. That dance had me feeling confused, aroused, bothered. What was Ravi trying to prove? And why did he rush off like that?

Suddenly, I felt a hand grasp my shoulder. With a quick twist, I had the man pressed against the wall of a building with his arm twisted painfully behind his back and my pistol to his head.

"Woah, woah, Emelia, holy shit! It's me, William!" I released him and holstered my pistol, embarrassed and flustered. "I... I'm sorry."

"I just wanted to make sure you were ok, but I guess so. Geez..." He straightened his coat and turned to walk back to the club, muttering, "Fucking psycho" under his breath. I sat down on the curb to collect myself, feeling in that moment like an actual fucking psycho. Then I heard Ravi laughing. I looked around and he was leaning against the corner of the building with his arms crossed laughing at what he just saw. I rolled my eyes and accepted his hand to help me up.

"I thought you left with the blond?" I asked angrily.

"No, just walked her to her car and wished her goodnight. She was boring, she only wanted to do shots and take pictures of herself," he frowned. "I thought I would come check on you, but it looks like you have it all under control," he smirked.

"Why are you checking on me?"

He cocked his head at me. "Don't you know? The Philippines are full of sex traffickers, it's a dangerous place." He said this with complete seriousness. We started laughing so hard I snorted, which made us laugh even harder.

We took the ferry to the resort and he insisted on walking me to my villa. At the entry to the resort, we saw a Filipino woman, scantily clad, flirting with an American tourist. We both knew what was going down but continued walking silently past them.

"Ugh, when will this all end? How much more do we have to do before it finally stops?" I said angrily.

"Mia, it will never end. It's just a dark part of humanity. But there's no end to it."

"Eventually it has to, people will get the point if we continue what we're doing," I said.

He shook his head. "What, do we continue doing this into our eighties? No, we just do what we can now and hope it makes a difference for somebody. There are some things we just can't control." He paused. "When Nera died, her mother came to the funeral with all of her terrible family. They... they screamed at me, in front of my daughter's casket, telling me it was my fault what happened to her. It was horrific. I believed it for a long time. That somehow, I had caused it. Eventually, I came to realize that horrible things happen, they just happen, and we can't stop them. They weren't aiming for Nera or her daycare center, it was all just chance. And we can't control it and we can't always stop it. I found peace after I realized that."

We had reached my villa, and I was glad to see the billowing curtains from the sides of the bedroom. Room service had remembered to leave them open for me.

"But how… how do you accept that? How can you be OK with such horrible things in the world and just live your life as if they aren't happening?"

He walked with me through the curtains into the dimly lit room. "Mia, the only way I found is to live for right now, for this moment. Because, in reality, it's all we have. And it's the only way we will ever truly find happiness through all the mess."

I slipped off my shoes and looked directly at him. *Live for right now, this moment.*

"This moment?" I asked him softly as I walked closer to him. My heart was racing.

He took a step closer to me. "Yes," he said quietly, gazing directly into my eyes.

"Were you dancing with me like that just to irritate William?" I had to know. And I had to know now.

"No… I… I danced with you like that because I wanted to. I've always wanted to."

Suddenly, our bodies met and he kissed me gently, caressing my hair and holding me close to him. My arms wrapped around his neck and I kissed him back, hungry for him, for more. He picked me up by my thighs and wrapped my legs around him, carrying me to the soft king bed. We fell into the bed, kissing more fiercely now, and tugging at each other's clothes. When all of our clothes were on the floor, he stopped, admiring my body, and leaned close to my ear whispering something in Hebrew as he ran his hand down the length of my body, the swell of my breast, the curve of my waist, and stroked my inner thigh gently making me tremble. He kissed my neck as he did this, touching my body as though every part of it were precious to him.

He said something else in Hebrew and leaned close to my

face, looking me directly in the eyes as he eased himself into me slowly. "Oh, Mia," he sighed. I breathed something between a gasp and a sigh, and he smiled as he began rhythmically moving his hips and kissing me. His touch was so familiar that every part of this just felt so... right. He ran his hands up the length of my arms, intertwining his hands with mine and holding them over my head as he thrust into me making me moan. Something was building inside me, something intense and powerful. I wrapped my legs around him, wanting every part of me to touch every part of him. His beautiful Hebrew words in my ear combined with his lips gently kissing my neck was building on that intensity and suddenly I was ravenous. I arched my back into him and wrapped my arms around him, digging my nails into his back. I cried out as I felt the most powerful and overwhelming pleasure of my entire life. He growled in my ear and pushed into me harder, increasing the pleasure to the absolute brink. Then, like a wave cresting in the ocean, I felt a release. My arms fell back on the bed and he changed his rhythm to a deliciously slow pace.

"What did you just do to me, Ravi?" I asked breathlessly.

He looked at me curiously, "Mia, that was an orgasm! Was... was that your first?"

I thought I had experienced orgasms before, but this was something entirely different. I had never felt the intensity, the release, the *power.* "I think so," I giggled.

Ravi leaned in close and whispered, "Want me to do it again?" He smiled that famous mischievous Ravi smile. "Oh, God, yes, do it again!"

We laughed about this and I rolled on top of him as he teased me about it some more. Our laughter could be heard from outside the billowing curtains, as the moon rose over the white sand of the beach and illuminated the ocean, which produced wave after wave in never ending constancy.

15

For the first time in my life, tourist week was an actual vacation. Ravi and I didn't see much of the group, we ventured off on our own and spent every minute together. The resort offered a guided tour to a waterfall, but Ravi located it on their map and insisted we find it for ourselves. "We are adventurers, Mia, we don't need guides!" he said grandly. We spent hours hiking through the dense jungle, but it was truly an adventure. Ravi had an innate sense of direction, so he led the way, and we would stop periodically to admire a flower or unusual plant or to just enjoy the strange and exotic place we found ourselves in at that moment. We finally found the stream fed by the waterfall and followed it to a wide, deep pool of beautifully clear water surrounded by dense green foliage. It could've been a photo straight out of a brochure. The waterfall was maybe thirty feet tall and straight down, with several enormous rocks looming out of the water. We stripped down to our swimsuits and jumped straight into the pool with no reservations. We swam under the waterfall, shocked by its immense power and the roaring sound of the water. The water was cool, though, and the hike had been hot so we took our time, which in itself felt luxurious to me. There was no rush, nothing keeping us from loving this exact moment and enjoying it as long as we wanted. Eventually, we climbed on the rocks and laid together on the warm, hard surface, listening to the waterfall and the birds in the surrounding trees, feeling the warm sun dry our skin.

We took what Ravi called a "shortcut" to get back to the

resort. According to the map, the guide led tourists back up a path similar to ours. However, Ravi found that if we climbed a cliff to the south of the waterfall it would put us within minutes of the resort. "Free climbing cliffs can be dangerous," he grinned at me as he said this.

"Life is dangerous," I shrugged, and started climbing the relatively sheer cliff. Finding each hand and foothold, I was able to think nothing of the task and reached the top to look down and see Ravi gaping at me. I was exhilarated and free, that climb shook off years of caution and anxiety.

He met me at the top and I embraced him and kissed him passionately. He laughed, "Mia, Mia, Mia…" shaking his head. He threw his arm over my shoulders and we took the short walk back to the hotel.

The beach right outside my villa was our favorite place for this vacation. We spent several days just lying in the sun, his head in my lap, listening to the waves. We talked about things we had never talked about. He told me of his childhood in Israel, how his mother made every effort to be there with him when she could, but when she couldn't she provided him with material comfort. "Computer systems and video games, to be exact." He said he started his career in computer engineering out of sheer curiosity and frankly, obnoxiousness. "She gave me every gaming system there was, but I figured out how to win the games quickly so I started to think about how the system worked." He disassembled his first PlayStation, just to see how it worked, and his mother was furious. "There was no stopping me after that," he laughed explaining how he took apart any and everything just to see how it worked. His mother learned to tolerate his curiosity, provided he figure out how to put it back together and make it work again. That same unruliness followed him into the high-end private schools his mother sent him to, he whizzed through the work getting perfect grades but driving his teachers insane with his nonstop curiosity and cocky attitude. He reprogrammed software in the computer lab to allow inappropriate content, hacked vending machines, rewired the lighting system to confuse the teachers, and when he hacked the grade tracking system to change his friend's grades the administration considered expulsion. "Mother wasn't having that, of course. She insisted that since I already had all the necessary credits for graduation, they let me graduate early and be rid of me." He shook his head, "She can be very pushy," and he smiled at that memory. He did, indeed, graduate early and spent his time in IDF before whizzing through MIT. I knew he was a prodigy but hearing about his childhood and being such a... well, a nerd showed me a different Ravi.

We swam in the ocean, napped on the beach, held hands as we walked to the bar, argued politics, I told him stories of growing up in Kansas, my marriage to Bryce and the divorce, we did anything but talk about the upcoming mission or any of our missions. But this mission coming up was looming over us, since we were walking in without a plan. We decided to let it rest and simply not think about it during the week, an idea I once would've thought terribly irresponsible but at this point, I didn't want to think about the mission. I only wanted to live in the moment with Ravi and soak up everything about him. He had a whole different life outside our missions that I've only merely glimpsed, so this vacation I learned who Ravi Weiss was as a human being.

But the lovemaking... oh, the lovemaking. Before Ravi I had an entirely different concept of sex. With Bryce it had been mechanical almost, very little foreplay and focused on the finish.

It was enjoyable for me sometimes, but toward the end of our marriage it had become a chore. And I did take the plunge once with Jonathan before our disastrous range date. It had been as one would expect, polite, but boring. Now, Ravi and I couldn't seem to get enough of each other. I felt like a hormone-fueled teenager discovering sex for the first time. We visited my villa two to three times a day, barely able to contain ourselves long enough to make it to the bedroom. He loved to take his time, he enjoyed my body, and he loved the effect his touch had on me making me tremble or cry out. He reveled in my pleasure, never leaving me unsatisfied or feeling like I wasn't cherished. He always whispered beautiful Hebrew things in my ear and would hold my hands and connect in a way that was beyond physical while we were in the moment. It was a holistic experience, I felt connected to Ravi emotionally, spiritually, physically. And, what's more powerful, is I learned to experience the world for the first time as a sexual being, a sexual woman. It was tremendously empowering, and I felt that confidence seep into my existence and begin a process of change in who I was as a person.

Our last night at the resort, we met with the group for the last time and had dinner together. Ravi and I sat together, sitting close and giggling to one another. Hannah McBride chimed in, "Well, we haven't seen much of you two this week. What have you been doing?"

Ravi leaned back in his seat and looked across the table at William and said, "We decided to spend a little alone time together, so I could learn *everything* about this spectacular woman. And believe me, it was worth it," he smiled at the group and grabbed my hand on the table. There were a few "Aaws" from the ladies and Mr. McBride actually winked at Ravi, but Mark, Julia, and William seemed unimpressed. Diana actually

148

stood up and walked out. It hurts being rejected by a man like Ravi, I couldn't blame her.

We finished dinner and all went our separate ways, but as we were walking out the Saito's stopped us and put our hands together and he smiled at us both, "This is good," he said "we have fifty years together. Seeing this, this is good." He patted our clasped hands and walked back to his room with his wife.

After a mind-blowing session of lovemaking, I laid next to Ravi, my head propped up on one hand, my other hand running over his chest, gently tracing the familiar course of scars from the years of missions we had been on together. "Ravi, I want you to tell me about what happened in Dubai."

"Are you sure you want to hear this? I thought you'd want to forget that mission altogether."

"Yes, I'm OK now. Tell me."

He told me about taking the truck back to the club. He walked in and searched for clues and found my blue scarf on the staircase leading downstairs. That's when he knew I was in trouble. "Lucky for us, when I took the security tape, I just tossed it in the passenger seat of the truck. So, I was able to pull it out and see the footage from the ground floor." He went through the footage carefully and saw my unconscious body being carried out and didn't know if I was dead or alive. "I had to push that thought out of my brain and focus on finding you, so I called the team and chartered a plane first." He had started using facial recognition to identify the Russian. When the bartender came into the bar to start his shift, Ravi tackled him and "pressed him" for information.

"Pressed him?" I asked.

"Well… he may be missing a few teeth, but he was very cooperative after I removed the third." Ravi shrugged. I

149

shuddered. He told Ravi who the Russian was and that he had been given the VIP room for his little "party". Ravi found out where he was staying and began to tell me the rest, but I stopped him.

"Between your mother and Hassan, I think I know how the rest played out. I have questions, though." I said seriously.

"Ok, I have answers," he laid back on the pillow and smiled.

"We've always had an agreement not to give ourselves or each other up and not to go back if one of us disappears. Why did you break protocol? It was very risky!" I had wondered that since Dubai.

"Of course it was risky, but I didn't know if you were dead or alive. I couldn't leave you to whatever they would do to you if you were alive."

"Why? That's part of the plan!"

"Mia... it wasn't *that* risky." He seemed unsure about that statement. I cocked my head and narrowed my eyes at him. "Ok, it was risky, but I need you," he said. That statement stunned me, I sat up quickly, looking away. "I mean, do you know how long it would take to train a replacement? I don't have time for that, and we have missions to do." I looked at him incredulously but he was laughing. He pulled me into his arms and kissed the top of my head as I nuzzled into the crook of his shoulder (my favorite place) and fell asleep.

Manila

We didn't bother seeing the travel group off at the airport. The dynamic had changed and we both knew somehow that our time with them had come to an end. We needed to get to our villa on the outskirts of Manila to start planning, and we had both been dreading this all week. The car ride was fairly quiet, we were both shifting to mission mode and trying to figure out how we were going to make this work. The first thing we did when we arrived, instead of laying out and preparing our gear, was cover the dining room table with maps, photos, reports and anything that may give us an idea. Ravi opened up his laptop and downloaded the latest sat photos while I started a pot of coffee. I brought him a cup and kissed him on the cheek while he reached up and caressed my face then sat down and started working. We pored over the material for hours, bringing up ideas, then shutting them down. This whole mission was a logistical nightmare and none of our usual tactics would work at all. We called it a night around three and went to bed together, exhausted and frustrated.

The next day we began again, thinking a fresh start might give us newer and better ideas. By lunch we were even more frustrated than before and no closer to the solution. Ravi picked up some takeout from a local place and we tried to talk through it.

"We could do it like Thailand," he said hopefully. "Turn it into multiple missions, several days?"

I swallowed a bite shaking my head. "No, won't work here. They're too widespread and the transport to the main island would require too much. There are only so many people you can fit in a speedboat."

"Not to mention, we're running out of time. When did you tell your USAID people to be ready?"

"I dropped a tip that something big would be happening this week and they needed extra manpower and supplies in Manila, but I was short on the specifics. We can call later when it's done, but we can't leave them hanging. We have to deliver." I didn't want to ruin our ties with this group, even though it was anonymous, I wanted them to take tips seriously.

Ravi nodded his head somberly and picked up a local report

about the island. We continued to brainstorm for hours more and seemed to reach a stalemate. We had been snapping at each other and accomplishing nothing, so I decided to take a break. I stood up, stretched, and went to the kitchen to make yet another pot of coffee. Ravi downloaded more sat photos and as he waited for them, he stood up and began pacing the room with his hands clasped behind his head. I sat back down, and he began thinking out loud.

"Ok, we have twelve clubs on the island with no idea how many women we can bring back from each."

"Yes," I said. I didn't want to interrupt his process.

"House to house to take out the perpetrators wouldn't help any of the women so that's out."

"Yes."

"We can't just load them up on a boat because there would be too many and too many places to gather them from."

"Yes." He was either seeing this as hopeless or was on to something.

"So, we need to figure out how to get them to come to us. Somehow…"

Not a bad idea, but it still had all the logistical glitches. Not enough transport, too much law enforcement at the docks, not enough time to get the word out…

"That's it! Yes! I got it!" Ravi exclaimed as he was looking at the new sat photos. I jumped up to see what he was looking at that excited him so much. Nothing looked much different to me.

He suddenly started shuffling frantically through all my reports about the different gangs in Manila. He found one in particular and flipped through until he found what he was looking for. He shoved it at me, "Look, Mia! This yacht belonging to the leader of one of the big Filipino gangs is parked right outside the north side of Mindoro island right now! He's taking a vacation and picking up women or whatever on the island!"

He led me to the laptop and zoomed in on a yacht. Sure enough, it was the exact yacht from the intel report. He clapped his hands and laughed, "Yes!" I wasn't following what this yacht had to do with anything.

"But what does that have to do with all this? How does that help us at all?"

He rubbed his hands together like an evil villain and grinned at me. I smiled in spite of myself, I loved when he was on a roll. "It will be our transport. We spread the word tomorrow that I want to have a big party on the yacht, lots of women, and the pimps just bring them to us!"

Hmmm... "Ok, that sounds great, but how in the hell do we get the yacht?"

"We just take it. Like pirates!" He thrust his hand in the air. I was beginning to think he had lost it, but he sat me down and showed me the topography of the island close to where the yacht was docked, and it was perfect for sniping. The security stays on the top decks of the yacht while the boss has his private parties below deck. He boards, I snipe, and we take out all the security. Then I board and help him take out whoever is on the lower decks and BOOM, we have a yacht. It made sense, if it all worked perfectly, but there were a lot of risks involved.

"This isn't Haitian street gangs, though, you're talking about a high-level boss. High level of security, lots of risks, not to mention, we'll be marked forever." I wasn't sure this was at our level; this could get us in over our heads.

"But the yacht can only hold so many people comfortably. He thinks he's safe because he's on his home turf, so his security won't be as tight. And, a BIG bonus, he does an enormous amount of human trafficking in this area. If we are serious about this, it's time to start taking the serious risks." Ravi seemed confident.

I considered this. It would be a big score, not just in the number of women saved but in ridding the world of the scum who make it happen. It was ambitious, sure, but we've had lots of successful missions and, to be honest, we were good at what we did.

"You'll have to cut their comms early," I said.

"Of course," he waved a hand dismissively, "that's simple."

"But what do we do when we get the yacht?"

Ravi sat down at the table and took both my hands in his. He laid out the details of the "party" and a rough timeline of how we could get it done. Once all the pimps were handled and the women boarded, we would literally drive into Manila Bay and leave the yacht anchored close enough that our contacts could board and pick up the women easily, but far enough out so we could still make a getaway. Once we got to the bay, the rest would be easy.

"We need to start prepping now. Meet me at the airport at four p.m." He started listing the things we would need, and we split up the tasks so we could get it all done before four. There was even more prep to do at the island so we would have to hurry. I hated doing things last minute, but this last-minute plan was solid, *if* there weren't so many *if's* involved.

16
Puerto Galera
Island of Mindoro, Philippines

The Manila preparations were fairly simple, Ravi secured us a motorcycle and stashed it at the beach of a remote fishing village outside the city. I found a nearby motel, not our usual beachside villa, but since it was only a couple of nights it would work. Once we arrived at Puerto Galero, Ravi found us a simple cottage outside the city, and we did a quick layout of our equipment. "We'll need everything this time. Don't go easy on ammo, you'll need plenty just to be safe." Once our equipment was prepped and ready, I quickly researched a nearby watersports store where I could find the rest of our supplies. When I finished, I looked up and my jaw dropped. The Ravi I knew had disappeared and, in his place, stood a seedy looking rich tourist. He had slicked back his curly hair with copious amounts of gel which made him look older and nefarious, somehow. He wore one of his designer suits, which usually look fantastic on him, but he had a red silk shirt underneath with an open collar and a fat gold chain around his neck. He even wore gold rings.

"Wow… now that's the right look for this," I said, a little creeped out by his new look.

He did a quick spin, then leaned closer to me, "Let's go for a ride in my Maserati, sweetheart," intentionally embellishing his Israeli accent and winked. I laughed and grabbed his face for a kiss. He kissed me back then laughed, buttoning his shirt sleeves.

"I will be out late for this part, can you handle the equipment and recon?" he asked.

I raised an eyebrow at him, "Really?" I asked.

He just smiled and left for all the Puerto Galero clubs. He was to talk to all the owners, throw money around a little, and hype up this big party on the yacht (that we didn't have yet) for tomorrow night. I said a little prayer for him and flagged down a jeepney to take me to the sport shop.

Fortunately, the owner of the watersport shop spoke English, which made our transaction so much easier. I arrived just before closing time, but he was a salesman to the core and totally bought my story about my husband and I wanting to explore the reefs. He gathered up wetsuits, waterproof backpacks, and promised to bring two inflatable skiffs with electric motors to White Beach for me tomorrow afternoon. I thanked him enthusiastically and took a jeepney back to the cottage to prepare for tonight's recon.

The yacht was anchored a few hundred meters off the shore of White Beach, which was illegal, but this man basically built the sex tourism industry on Mindoro, so he was given certain privileges that came with such notoriety. I had climbed the hill from the interior of the island and crawled to the edge to make sure I wasn't spotted. I set up my scopes and looked for security on the outer areas of the yacht. Ravi was right about that part, a dozen or so security guys wandered around the sundecks but looked relaxed, having drinks together and joking among themselves. Not once did I see one scan the island for snipers during my entire three-hour recon. That reassured me that perhaps this was possible after all. Then the boss man came up the stairs from a lower deck wearing a bathrobe. I expected the security team to stiffen up, but the Boss just poured a drink and joked around with them for about fifteen minutes before descending the stairs for the night and most of the yacht's lights turned off. Feeling emboldened, I crouched and walked to the very edge of the hill so see if I could climb down quickly tomorrow night and it was all sand, no problems there. This recon supported everything Ravi said, so I packed up my gear and walked back to the cottage. Ravi still wasn't back, so I took off my clothes to get some much-needed sleep before tomorrow's work.

I heard the door open around three-thirty and grabbed my pistol from the nightstand. Ravi gently opened the bedroom door and jokingly held his hands up, "I thought you would be sleeping, but I underestimated you," he said with a grin.

"How did it go?" I asked sleepily.

"Perfect, perfect. I used their rivalry against them. I told them I would be asking all the bar owners to bring their finest 'products' so it would almost be like an auction. I don't know what the final number will be, but if they all show it could be big for us." He yawned as he took off his suit and jewelry. "These men disgust me; I despise pretending to work with them." He sat down on the bed and I crawled up behind him wrapping my arms around his chest and kissing his neck. He immediately relaxed and reached back to run his hands up my thighs. And we connected again, in that way that only Ravi can give me, making me feel as though we were one. That night we embraced each other all night as we slept, finding comfort in each other as we faced the grim uncertainty of tomorrow.

It was noon before we finally got out of bed. Taking our time was a luxury, but we wanted to enjoy it while we had the chance. Ravi kissed me and went to shower, while I made us a light brunch. We packed our waterproof backpacks with the necessary gear for the mission then stashed them in an enormous beach bag for our cover. For my beach bag, I cut two small circles in the side with a razor blade and slid the scopes in, so they were barely noticeable. We dressed in tourist beach wear, Ravi whistling at me in my bikini and sunhat. "A swimsuit like *that* certainly won't make you blend in," he joked, eyeing me hungrily. I laughed and wrapped a sari around my waist as we headed to the beach.

As promised, the watersports salesman had provided two inflatable skiffs which were at the bottom of the hill I intended to use as a sniper's perch after sunset. We set up our surveillance camp a few meters down the beach, a big umbrella, towels, beach chairs, and Ravi pretended to work on his laptop while I pretended to read a book. I sat my bag next to me with the scopes facing the yacht and toggled the switch for Ravi to control the zoom. He had a perfect view of what was happening on the yacht and we could recon for hours like this.

"It looks like fairly light security, you were right. I don't see any children or family, just four men meeting on the upper deck right now." He was watching their every move. "Oh, now the women have come out from below deck, they're turning this into a party!" He laughed. We knew that if the gangsters partied all afternoon they may not be as prepared for our raid.

"How many crew have you seen?" I asked.

He watched for a few moments, "I know there's a captain in there somewhere, probably a couple of kitchen workers." We hadn't discussed that part, but we'll have to handle that when we board. I dozed off for a little while and woke to Ravi still monitoring the gangster's movements.

"Sorry, did I miss anything good?"

"Drunk gangsters, naked women, hot tubs... just normal surveillance stuff," he grinned at me and I laughed. "At least we got one more day on the beach together," he said, and he kissed me intensely. The sun was due to set in an hour, so we packed up our gear and headed off the beach and up the hill. We both put on our wetsuits and backpacks and reviewed the plan a couple more times. I had the feeling Ravi was nervous; he was joking too much and laughing a little too hard. With all the complexities of this mission, there was a lot that could go wrong; we had contingencies, but they seemed more like good intentions than actual plans. Also, there was the added unspoken concern that our changed relationship may somehow compromise the mission.

The sun set over the hill and dusk settled in. Fifteen more minutes until go time. I carefully strapped Ravi's Kevlar vest around him, ensuring the emergency release was accessible. He did the same for me and we double checked our weapons and gear... again.

"Do you have enough mags? I don't want you to run out of ammo." I asked him.

"Plenty." He sighed looking at the yacht then looked at me. He stared silently into my eyes for a moment then kissed me. "So, I'll see you on *our* yacht in about ten minutes?" He laughed.

"I'll be there. You just be careful... bail if you need to and let me handle it from up here," I said, pleading with my eyes.

"Pssh, Eleora Weiss did not raise a quitter!" He winked at me and climbed down the hill to the little skiff to make his way to the yacht.

I sighed. Time to get to work. I set up my sniper position and watched him as he sped along the water, the electric motor almost silent and leaving only a small wake. He quickly docked at the swim platform and I lost sight of him as he ascended the stairs to reach the middle deck. He quickly took out two security guards, so I started taking out the ones I could see, beginning with the men closest to Ravi. I had taken out about six when I lost sight of Ravi again as he was on the starboard side and the cabin blocked my view. I saw no more security on the outer decks. I worried that something had happened but he appeared and radioed me, "Outer decks secure." I breathed a sigh of relief. I disassembled my sniper rifle quickly and slung my AR-15 over my back and slid down the sandy hill to get to the skiff as quickly as possible.

I was docking at the swim platform within minutes and Ravi met me there pulling security while I boarded. He led me through the middle deck to check for more security, but we found that they were travelling extremely light on security. On the upper deck, near the galley and the cockpit we saw just the captain, but he hadn't noticed anything awry yet, so we decided it was time to go below deck and take out the gangster. Ravi led the way down the small staircase and we immediately took down the two guards waiting outside the double doors to what we guessed was a suite of some sort. I kicked the doors open and we saw four high-level Filipino gang leaders passed out on the couches of what looked like an office. We looked at each other and laughed at this crazy good luck and executed the gang leaders. We pulled the bodies of the security guards into the office and closed the doors.

"Well, then... that was easy," Ravi said with a huge grin. "Maybe we should change our specialty to piracy!"

We headed to the cockpit and Ravi strode in with his pistol held on the captain, who immediately held up his hands. "No, no, no, I just drive! Only drive! They pay me, I drive, I know nothing!" He was shaking and switching back and forth between Tagalog and English as he begged for his life. "My family! Please!"

"Will you work for us now instead?" Ravi said calmly, passing him an envelope full of money.

The captain's eyes widened looking in the envelope. He stopped to count it and laughed. "I'll drive you around the world for this kind of money! I get my family out of Manila, maybe I buy a farm, who knows? I could buy a yacht myself!" He cackled at his own joke. Ravi and I looked at each other, not as amused as the captain was.

"Puerto Galera, not the docks. Somewhere a little more private." Ravi was using his intimidation voice and it worked. The captain (who later told us his nickname was Gus, among other details about his life) immediately started the engines and pulled the anchor. It looked like we had an ally.

"Let's get rid of the bodies and get this place cleaned up," I said. We couldn't have a party on a blood splattered yacht.

We disposed of the bodies and while Ravi was changing into a rich playboy, I found a water hose and began spraying down the decks to get rid of the blood splatter. Ravi ascended the steps in shorts, a horrific Hawaiian shirt halfway unbuttoned and the same jewelry and hair from the night he went to the clubs. The effect was startling, but perfect. He looked like the perfect sleazy rich guy. He saw me with the water hose and shouted, "Ahoy, wench, swab the deck!" making himself laugh hysterically.

"Oh no," I said behind a suppressed smile, "we will NOT be talking like pirates this whole mission."

He laughed some more, "But we are pirates, someday you'll admit it." He took the hose from me so I could go prepare for the next stage of the mission.

I did a cursory search of the galley and storage areas to make sure we didn't have any extra crew hiding. It was a little strange, such a small crew, but I was grateful that we didn't have that added complication. The galley was enormous, and when I looked in the huge commercial refrigerator, I found four large trays of simple local finger foods, probably from a caterer so the gangster didn't have to bring a kitchen crew. The first tray had been picked over, but at least there were enough provisions for the women during our trip to Manila Bay. The storage, or pantry, area had plenty of dry goods and had a row of clean white pants and smocks for the crew. This luck was perfect, so I pulled the smock and pants over my wetsuit and pulled my hair back into a sleek ponytail. I searched through a cabinet to make sure I could find champagne flutes and a big enough tray. Then I pulled a baggie of white powder out of my backpack and put it in a drawer in the galley while stashing my backpack in the storage area. Everything was ready.

Ravi checked in with Gus and after a lengthy conversation, because *everything* is a lengthy conversation with Gus, they decided on a small dock just south of the main docks that wouldn't be patrolled as much by law enforcement. Ravi immediately began texting his contacts from the clubs, who were eager to bring their "products" and make some serious money. We each had our pistols on us, concealed just in case and waited on the upper deck in the luxurious sun chairs. "This is going well so far," he commented.

"I know, I'm just waiting for something bad to happen, taking the yacht was too easy," I said with a chuckle. He just smiled and grabbed my hand when he heard the first ding from his phone.

"Are we ready?" I nodded and followed him to meet our passengers and victims on the middle deck.

17

"Welcome, friends! So glad you could make it!" Ravi gushed as the first group arrived on the yacht. He commented on the quality of the women as they walked past him, telling the men they did well and handing them each an envelope. The men stared in awe at the sheer luxury of the yacht and seemed very satisfied with this arrangement. He invited them to go to the upper deck while he met with the next group, who was already walking down the dock. It looked like we had forty women already between the two groups, and I met the women at the middle deck and led them downstairs to a long room called a saloon, with a bar, couches, even a dance floor. At the end of the saloon was a dining room with a half a dozen tables, then doors to the different staterooms at the very back of the dining room. There was plenty of room for the women to get comfortable, but as more arrived it would get tight. We would just have to deal with that as it came, because Ravi was already welcoming a third group, so I had to play the pleasant and gracious crew member. Within an hour we had fifteen men aboard on the upper deck and almost three hundred women packed into the lower deck. The women looked concerned, so I started some music and tried to make them comfortable.

"Does anyone speak English?" I asked hopefully.

"I do." A tiny woman wearing a skin-tight pink dress stepped up to me. "Whatchu want, sweetie?"

"What's your name?" I asked her.

"My name is Queen, honey, what's yours?" she was

definitely playing the part.

"No, your real name," I looked her right in the eyes.

Her shoulders dropped and she sighed. "Rosa. Seriously, what do you want?" Her entire demeanor changed, accent, stance, everything. I wondered if I could trust her.

"How long have you been doing this, Rosa?" I asked.

"Six damn years. Why? What do you care?" She was getting defensive; I didn't want to lose her.

"I may need your help with some things tonight, and you seem like a leader. Can I trust you?"

"Well, that depends on what you need and what I get out of it." Fair enough.

"First, can you keep everyone calm since it's so crowded, I don't speak Tagalog." I was hoping to start small and bring her the big stuff later.

"No problem." She nodded. She began to yell at the group in Tagalog, and they seemed to respect her so I started to think she may be the person I needed for this job.

"Thanks," I said and closed the doors. I started toward the upper deck where I could hear all the men laughing. Ravi had opened an expensive bottle of scotch to get everyone relaxed and it seemed to be doing the job. Everything was going according to plan so far.

I stepped onto the upper deck and put my hands behind my back. "Excuse me, sir, just checking to see if the gentlemen need any refreshments." Ravi stood up and gestured toward me with his glass, "Get these men some champagne, they're my guests tonight and will be staying for the party and they deserve a toast for all the fine party favors they provided!" This was met with cheers from the men, who were a little drunk already. Perfect.

I walked to the galley and pulled out fifteen champagne

flutes and set them neatly on the tray. I pulled out my baggie, it was filled with Xanax that Ravi scored on his night on the town and I had crushed the pills to a fine powder. I spooned a near lethal dose into each champagne flute before grabbing a couple of the dozens of bottles stored in the liquor cooler. I filled each glass to the brim and stirred them gently. I placed the tray on a server's cart and rolled it onto the deck, giving each man a glass, except Ravi. Ravi held up his glass of scotch and toasted the men enthusiastically and chugged what remained of his drink. The men, not wanting to be outdone, did the same. This part of the plan had been all Ravi's and I thought it was either brilliant or idiotic, but seeing it play out exactly as he said showed me just how well he understood the bravado of men.

I stepped into the cockpit to update Gus, who was reading a fishing magazine. "Gus, in exactly thirty minutes I need you to start the engines and get us straight to Manila Bay," I told him.

"Yes, ma'am," he gave me a jaunty salute. "You sure you don't want me to take you around a little? We have lots of islands, pretty stuff, up north there's waterfalls and beaches you wouldn't believe—"

I cut him off, "No, straight to Manila Bay." I started to walk out, but turned around, "Maybe you can go there for yourself when you get your own yacht," I said with a smile.

He laughed, "Yes! Take the kids, see the world!" He was still laughing as I walked out of the cockpit and down to the lower deck.

I took off the smock and pants so I was in my wetsuit. I put my Kevlar vest back on and my backpack, in case things went south. I wanted everything with me if I needed to do... well, anything outside of the plan. I waited outside the doors of the saloon until Ravi radioed me, "All fifteen are out." The Xanax had knocked them all unconscious, maybe even killed them but I wasn't concerned with that part right now. I pulled a carefully typed note out of my backpack and walked into the saloon.

Rosa met me at the door. She said everyone was calm, just wondering when the party was starting. I told her there was no party and handed her the note. It read:

You are not being kidnapped, we are taking you to Manila to reunite with your families.

There is a group there that is safe that can help you find work to support your families and give you money to help.

If you want to leave, do it now. Just know, there will be no work for you here since all the club owners are dead.

Rosa read the note quickly, her eyes widening at every line. "Is this for real?" She asked. "What group is this?"

"It's real. The group is USAID, they already know you are coming." I was hoping she would read the note to the rest of the women.

Rosa shook her head for a moment. "You know, you didn't have to word it so simply. I'm educated, three years at university. Why do you think I know English so well?" She stood a little taller as she told me this.

"How did this happen to you? You could've graduated by now!" I asked, genuinely shocked and curious.

She shrugged her shoulders, "When my father died my mother couldn't take care of my brothers and sisters alone." She gave me a knowing look, "When they brought me here, they said I would be a nanny for rich people. Ha!" She cackled and shook her head. "So, you want me to read this to the group before we leave for Manila, right? I got you." She sauntered straight into the middle of the saloon and started shouting in Tagalog. The women gasped, some cried, they all seemed to have questions and Rosa was doing her best to address those with questions. In all only thirteen women left the yacht. They walked out just as the engines roared to life and Gus steered us away from Mindoro

166

toward Manila. I saw them watching from the dock until we were out of sight and I often wondered if it was regret I saw on their faces that night.

After we were a few miles off the coast and in open water, we tossed the club owners overboard. Ravi changed into his wetsuit and secured his gear while I prepared the server's cart with all the caterer's trays from the fridge and a few cases of water. He came into the galley looking refreshed and excited, "Mia, this is working!" I saw his hopeful smile and said, "Come with me." We rolled the cart to the elevator that opened up into the dining room. His jaw dropped when he saw how many women were packed into the two rooms. He rolled the cart into the middle and I heard Rosa shouting something to the women. They all looked at Ravi and started clapping for him, for us. It was a long round of applause and Ravi blushed and grinned widely. He looked at me, eyes watering and we both just felt *good*. He ran a hand over his eyes quickly and gestured toward the cart before pulling me into the elevator. We went to the upper deck in silence, in awe, really.

We strolled casually to the bow of the yacht to the luxurious sundeck. He threw his arm around my shoulders as we watched the water.

"We should get a yacht," he said suddenly. I laughed at the thought of us having a yacht. "Oh, I almost forgot, I have a surprise for you!" He pulled off his backpack and pulled out his laptop and after fiddling with it for a few minutes, I hear the sweet sound of jazz trumpet. "I downloaded some Billie Holliday for you," he smiled and reached for my hand. "Now, that's how you ask a lady to dance," I said with a wink. He rolled his eyes and wrapped me in his warm familiar embrace, and we swayed along with the ocean, oblivious to the rest of the world as we quietly passed the dim outline of Corregidor Island and entered Manila Bay.

18

In the end, Ravi was right. Through all his cynical world views about everything happening by chance, it was chance that took us out. All our planning, research, and perfect execution amounted to basically nothing when the force of chance, or fate, if you prefer, took over and started a chain of events that were well beyond our control or knowledge.

Because, what we didn't (and couldn't) know, was that the rivalling gangs in Manilla were secretly planning and preparing for an all-out territory war. The drug trade was hot and both gangs wanted to control the majority of metro Manilla. We didn't know that the gangster that owned the yacht took a skeleton crew to Mindoro, not to party, but to have a top-secret planning session with his leadership on how they were going to completely obliterate the rival gang. That rival gang was also secretly planning a takeover in the heart of Manilla.

Because, when we slipped past the island of Corregidor, we didn't know that there was a small fishing boat headed to Mindoro at that exact moment. This normally wouldn't arouse any suspicion, but this particular fishing boat was carrying a shipment of heroin from the rival gang and was manned by three men who could easily recognize the outline of their rival's yacht. While Ravi and I danced on the bow, the men reported back to the gang leadership who began assembling a team.

And, because what the owner of the yacht knew, that we didn't know, was that cruising into Manilla Bay in his very recognizable yacht was something he would never do. He knew that he was a high-level target and purposely stayed away from the bay to avoid putting himself in an inescapable position that would likely get him assassinated.

I've gone over the events that followed too many times to count, trying to find a way that we could've done it differently or changed the outcome, but I always come back to the same answer. Just like sweet little Nera being a victim of a random rocket attack, chance was the winner. Some things we simply can't control no matter how hard we try, because the world has different plans for us and regardless of the outcome, the world just keeps turning.

Manilla Bay, Philippines

We danced for about forty-five minutes, but it only felt like a moment. I could've danced with Ravi like that forever. But, when the songs finished, he kissed me and went down to the swim platform to get the Wave Runners fueled up and ready for us to make our escape as we left the yacht in the bay. We could see the lights of Manilla and were getting close to where we planned to drop anchor. I had left my backpack with my cell phone on the middle deck so I walked casually toward the staircase to call my contact and let her know that the shipment had arrived. I was halfway down the staircase when a roaring blast threw me to the middle deck and, my ears ringing and heat coming in waves from the bow, I scrambled to my feet to see the bow of the yacht destroyed and in flames. I was shaking but uninjured wondering, *What the hell just happened?*

I sprinted to the swim platform to find Ravi and he was scrambling to get the lifeboats together. They were inflatable, one only had to pull a ring and they would pop open, so he was frantically popping them open and throwing them in the water, attaching them to each other with carabiners.

"Oh, thank God you're ok!" he gasped breathlessly. He told me he had glanced up at the coast at the right moment and saw the rocket come from a small peninsula on the east side of the bay. "I'm trying to get these damn life-boats together to evacuate, go get the women now, we need to get off the ship!" He was screaming these orders, in full panic mode. "No, I need to take out the shooter before he destroys all of us!" I started running up the stairs and I heard him screaming for me to stop but I wouldn't. He had given me a rough idea where the shooter was, I could maybe take him out and buy us more time. I snatched my backpack and climbed atop the cabin, hoping for a decent vantage point.

I laid prone with my rifle and scope, but it was hard to see with all the smoke and the swaying of the damaged yacht. I scanned the coastline until I miraculously saw the shooter, loading another round into his rocket launcher. I fired immediately, but missed. This alerted the shooter, who knelt down, still loading his round but now fumbling, trying to speed up the process. I waited until a wave of smoke passed then took another shot, watching it hit the tree right next to the shooter's head. "Come on!" I screamed at myself pulling the bolt back for another try. I tried to get a feel for the sway of the yacht and released a breath, firing one more time. This was a direct hit, but it was too late. The shooter fell facedown right after firing the rocket launcher.

Time seemed to slow down as the rocket hit directly in the middle of the starboard hull, destroying the cockpit and our Captain, Gus, and launching me back and into the air. I felt some shrapnel slice my cheek and remember thinking vaguely, *I lost my rifle.* The enormous wave of heat shoved me roughly into the water and another piece of shrapnel embedded itself into my right thigh. I was underwater in darkness and totally disoriented about which way the surface was. I panicked and started swimming, but realized I was swimming deeper into the bay. I tried to calm myself and looked for the light of the blazing ship and swam upward to it. I broke the surface and took a deep breath of acrid smoke and fuel fumes. I saw I wasn't too far from the yacht, so I swam as best I could in the Kevlar vest and with one leg fairly useless and finally reached the swim platform where Ravi was unloading frightened and screaming women into the lifeboats. He looked at me and gasped, "Are you ok, you need to sit down," my injuries must have looked worse than they felt. "No, I'm fine. How many boats?" I asked breathlessly.

"Ten," he looked at me grimly.

"That's not enough!" I ran past the line of women rushing to board the lifeboats, being thrown off balance by the shifting of the yacht, which was quickly taking water through the hole in the hull. I found Rosa at the door of the saloon helping women get out of the wreckage. The far end of the saloon had taken a direct hit with the last rocket; fire was blazing out of the doors of the staterooms and the entire saloon looked wrecked.

"Anyone left inside alive?" I asked her over the din.

"Maybe in the back, when the explosion happened, so many women were killed, it was terrible!" She was crying, but she was determined to help these women get to safety.

I helped her usher the last of the uninjured (or at least the walking injured) toward the boats and told her, "Go get on a boat now, there aren't enough and some women will just have to hang on to the sides. They need you safe so you can help them!" She nodded and dashed past the line of women. I took a deep breath and ran into the saloon to see if anyone was left that needed help getting out. Toward the back end of the room, it was mostly bodies, full of shrapnel. I heard screaming and went in deeper, trying to see through the smoke.

I looked down and stopped completely, stunned at what I had found. A woman was lying on the ground, dead, and the fire was approaching. Holding her hand was a small boy, maybe two or three, trying to wake her. He was screaming, "Mama! Mama!" *How did a child end up here? How did we miss that?* I scooped up the little boy and ran out the door. I took him to the platform and Ravi stopped handing out life jackets to the rest of the women who wouldn't fit on the boats and just stared for a moment.

"How?" he asked. I shook my head, not knowing how to answer that.

Ravi had made a sort of flotilla for the life-boats, attaching them in a circle and directing the women who wouldn't fit in the boats to wear life jackets and when those ran out, he told them to just hold the sides of the life-boats. They were in the middle of the flotilla, keeping them as safe as we could under the circumstances. The yacht suddenly lurched hard starboard, on the verge of completely tipping. "We have to go, now," Ravi said as he directed me to my Wave Runner. We got them in the water just as the swim platform became submerged with water. I drove around the flotilla with the child tucked in front of me, looking for Rosa.

I found her on one of the boats yelling at all the women, presumably to get down and make a lower profile in the water. I pulled up next to her and tried to hand the child to her.

"No, absolutely not." She shook her head and refused to take him from me.

"No, Rosa, you have to save him!"

"I'm responsible for all these women, if he comes with us, he'll make too much noise and we'll all be killed. I won't do it,

172

that's not my job," she said adamantly. She was right.

"You want him safe, you'll... you'll just have to save him yourself," she looked at me sympathetically.

The yacht finally tipped making an enormous groan as it began to sink into the bay. The women shrieked, though they were a safe distance from the wreckage. I reached out to Rosa and took her hand, not saying a word, just holding her hand for a moment in gratitude. Then I wrapped the child in my vest with me, strapping him tightly to my chest and sped to the west, following Ravi.

Through the noise of the sinking ship, the wailing of police sirens from the mainland, and the noise of the Wave Runner, I heard the distinct sound of small arms fire. We were being attacked, again. I leaned down low and sped faster, following Ravi's lead. Just before we reached the shoreline, I saw him veer wildly to the left for just a moment before recorrecting. *Did he get hit?* He made it to the shore where we had stashed the bike, so I thought he might be OK after all.

We climbed off the Wave Runners and Ravi took the boy so I could dismount. We sneaked into the trees and found a clearing where we could regroup. I realized at some point I must have put on my backpack, and I pulled it off grateful that I at least had the foresight to do that much.

"Were you hit?" I asked Ravi.

"No, no, it just clipped my Kevlar. I got lucky," he gave me a half-hearted smile. "Let me treat your wounds real quick, you're a mess." The boy sat placidly while Ravi applied steri-strips to my cheek and examined my leg. There were about four inches of exposed metal sticking out, I wasn't sure how deep it was, but I wasn't feeling much pain.

Ravi started to grab it, "No! It may be keeping me from

bleeding out! We need to leave it there until… well, until we can do something about it," I said, uncertain of when that might be. We wrapped gauze around it and taped it in place, but we both knew it would only buy us time. We gave the boy a quick examination, he seemed uninjured except for a small burn on the hand that was holding his mother's hand. He looked at me with tearful eyes and leaned into me, but he didn't scream or wail. My heart ached for him and for his loss.

"We have to go," Ravi said. "There may be police or gang members in the area soon."

"Wait!" I had almost forgotten the most important part of the mission. I pulled my phone out of my backpack and called my contact.

"The women are in life-boats in the bay, some don't even have life jackets. Please do what you can to help them before the police get to them," I said. Then I hung up before she could say anything. We had to ride to the safe house, which was several miles away, and we had to do this with a child, so I was mentally preparing myself for the next step.

We mounted the bike with the boy secured between Ravi and I. Ravi drove more carefully than usual, I'm guessing because of the boy. We were about halfway to the safe house when suddenly Ravi dropped the throttle and the bike lurched to a stop on the side of the road. He was breathing heavily and leaning over the handlebars. "Mia, I just…" then he collapsed on the ground.

Panicked, I set the boy down next to Ravi and ripped off his Kevlar to examine him. The bullet had not clipped his Kevlar, but rather it went right between the plates beneath his right arm and into his chest. I leaned closer and recognized it as a sucking chest wound, meaning his lung was collapsing, if it hadn't already. I dug though my backpack for my med kit and ripped it open. I cleaned the area as quickly as I could and placed an occlusive dressing with a one-way valve over the wound and waited. A moment later Ravi took a labored breath and seemed to rouse. He tried to sit up, and I helped him.

"Did you know you were shot?"

"Yes, but I thought we could make it to the safe house," he said through short breaths.

We needed to get somewhere safe, and quick. I helped Ravi to his feet and hoisted the boy onto my hip. I spotted a narrow opening with a small dirt road on the opposite side of the main road. Ravi needed to lean on me to walk, and we made slow progress, between his injuries and mine. The dirt road led down a steep hill and wound around to a small shack next to a stream with a couple of goats in the yard and numerous chickens. The sun was just coming up so I was able to scan for any danger, not that it would matter in our condition. I opened the door to the shack and saw a simple sleeping mat, a small homemade table with tools neatly arranged in pots, and a fireplace. I laid Ravi down on the sleeping mat and he either passed out or fell asleep immediately. I sat down across from the door with the boy and started digging through my backpack, looking for some morphine for Ravi and some burn cream for the boy. The boy climbed into my lap and wrapped his arms around my waist. I stopped, looking at this poor child who just wanted a little love in the face of all this scary stuff. I took off my Kevlar vest and wrapped my arms around him, rocking him naturally as I would with my own children.

Within five minutes he was sleeping soundly, his beautiful dark lashes laying on his full baby cheeks. I laid him down gently and went back to my backpack, when I heard the door open. I pulled the pistol out of my bag and turned quickly placing myself between the door and the child. A man stood in the door, wearing a wide straw hat, and dirty clothes with pants wet up to the knees. He was holding a simple fishing pole in one hand and a creel in the other. When he saw me, he dropped them both and put his hands up slowly. *"Quien eres tu?"* I was grateful he was one of the local Spanish speakers.

"Nosotros no te lastimaremos," I told him, or "We won't hurt you". I moved aside so he could see the boy and gestured to Ravi, then to the shrapnel sticking out of my leg. His eyes widened a little, but he just mumbled something in Spanish and ambled over to the fireplace to start a fire. I watched him warily, as he poured some water into a pot and retrieved his creel, pulling out several fish and lying them on the table. He cleaned each fish expertly and quickly, setting the meat aside. The man continued to slowly move about the cabin and I leaned back against the wall and closed my eyes, not sensing any danger from this man.

"Hambrienta?" I heard. I looked down and saw grilled fish and a bowl of rice. He sat a plate in front of the boy, who roused when he smelled breakfast. He took some to Ravi, but he was still sleeping, his labored breathing making me more nervous by the second. *"Gracias"* I said, and the boy and I ate. Halfway through our breakfast the boy said, "Milk?" I looked at him wide-eyed. He hadn't spoken a word since his rescue and now I find out he speaks English. The fisherman understood this and poured a small mug of goat's milk for the boy and handed it to him, smiling.

The boy drank every bit of the milk then set the mug down and smacked his lips and said, "Aaah. Yum!" The fisherman and I shared a laugh at this, I was just glad to see the boy coming around a little. We finished our meal in silence and I helped the fisherman clean up. I checked on Ravi. He was growing pale and sleeping heavily. *Where do we go from here?* I thought. The adrenaline had worn off and the pain from my injuries was wearing on me. I sat down next to the boy and leaned against the wall of the shack.

"*Senora, senora…*" I heard. I had fallen asleep and judging from the angle of the sun slanting through the small window of the shack, I had slept for a long time. I was feeling sore and feverish, the wound on my leg aching. The boy was sleeping on my chest, arms and legs draped around me. I laid the boy down, as he started to rouse, rubbing his eyes, and looked at the fisherman.

"*Tu amigo se esta muriendo*", and he pointed to Ravi. I checked on his wound and his breathing. It didn't look good, but I had no idea what to do for him. I think the fisherman was right, he was dying.

Suddenly, Ravi's eyes opened and he looked around the room. "Nera, darling, come see Papa," he said to the boy. The boy looked at me and I nodded. He walked over to Ravi, who wrapped an arm around him and began speaking to him in Hebrew with tears in his eyes. The little boy just laid his head on Ravi's shoulder and allowed him to cuddle him. Ravi gradually drifted off again, but the boy stayed there.

I thought about the protocol we had created in the beginning:
Never turn ourselves in.
Never go down without a fight.
Always stick to the story.
Never return for the partner.

Then I thought about the life I had in New Hampshire as I dug through my backpack for my phone. Jenna and Ethan would be OK with Laura and Bryce, but I thought about their wedding days, kissing their babies' perfect little faces, sharing their joy in becoming adults and parents, graduations, heartbreaks, successes and failures. I thought about all the people I would miss, the kids, Laura, my colleagues, Eleora, Ravi, Mom and Dad, Grandpa, the family farm. I had lived a good life and didn't want to miss anything that was to come, but some things are worth losing everything for. I handed the fisherman my phone with tears streaming down my face and begged, *"Policia, por favor."* He called and the boy came to me wiping my tears away saying, "It's ok, it's ok, no cry."

19

I leaned against the wall again, hoping to sleep until the police arrived. The fisherman was busy, he went to my bag and grabbed my pistol and put a hand on my forehead. He shook his head and I could see him through the door throwing the pistol in the stream and wetting a cloth. He came inside and laid the cool cloth on my head, which felt amazing, then hid my Kevlar vest in a basket covered with a woven blanket. Then he sat calmly in his chair with his rosary beads, reciting a prayer in Spanish. I found that very soothing and drifted off quickly.

I heard the police come into the shack but barely opened my eyes. The fever had taken hold and my entire body was aching. I watched them check Ravi and radio something in Tagalog. They tried to talk to me, and to the boy, but I didn't understand them and pulled the boy into my lap, desperately trying to protect him. Moments later the sirens from the ambulance wailed in the distance and I drifted off again as the police were checking Ravi for a pulse.

The ambulance ride was nothing more than a blur for me. I remember pointing the EMTs to Ravi and refusing to allow anyone to take the boy from me. Then I woke up in a cramped ambulance with the boy sitting on the bench holding my hand and I was holding Ravi's hand. The EMTs were working on Ravi furiously, I remember believing he was already dead and crying.

There are a few hazy memories from when we first arrived at the hospital, but they don't follow any logical order or make any sense. I think I was delirious with fever, I refused to allow the staff to take the boy because I believed he was Ethan at the time and may have even taken a swing at someone. I remember deep pain in the wound on my cheek but being somehow detached from that pain. I remember seeing a tiny little hand reaching through crib bars toward me, and touching the little fingers for comfort. Blurry images of doctors, nurses, bandages, hearing beeps and people speaking in different languages. Beyond that, I remember sleep. So much sleep.

One morning I awoke, dazed from the pain medication, but finally feeling somewhat alert. A doctor stood at my bedside, smiling patiently at me. He looked through my chart and said, "You are making excellent progress, Emelia. How do you feel?" I tried to sit up a little and felt a bolt of pain flash through my right leg. "Good, just pain in my leg." He nodded. "You had an infection, and the wound was deep enough to do some nerve damage and artery damage. We've repaired the wound, you'll have a scar of course, but with physical therapy you'll be able to walk again." He seemed quite happy with this outcome, so I assumed I should be as well. I looked over for the boy, he was no longer in the room with me. My heart sank, wondering where he was and if he was being cared for. Two nurses came in when the doctor left to help me stand up and try to walk with crutches, which took a little work, but I was able to manage. They wanted to discharge me the next day, wasting no time getting me out. I liked that.

When I settled back into bed, the nurses gave me another injection of pain medication and I was about to drift off to sleep when I heard a loud knock at the door and saw it swing open. A very official man in a suit, definitely not Filipino, strode into my room and straight to my bedside. He pulled up a chair.

"Hello, Dr. Burke, I'm Detective James Scott from Interpol.

We have a few questions for you, do you think you'll be able to answer those for me?" All business. I nodded my head and remembered the protocol: *Always stick to the story.*

"Good," he opened up a small notebook and clicked his pen very officially. "Can you tell me what happened in the bay?"

My mind was a little fuzzy from the medication but I thought, *Keep it simple, don't give too many details.* "We took the Wave Runners out early so we could watch the sun rise in the bay and a yacht exploded next to us. I was injured so we tried to get to shore, but there was gunfire and Ravi was shot. We tried to get back to our vacation rental, but Ravi couldn't make it. A very kind fisherman took us in until we felt it was safe enough to call the police." I didn't have to pretend to look frightened, I was wondering about Ravi and if he survived all this.

"And the boy, he isn't *your* son, correct?" I hesitated. "Correct."

The detective sighed and leaned back in his chair for a moment. There was an awkward silence during which I was grateful for the pain medication and the effect it had on my mind. "Well, your stories match up and everything looks just about right."

"He's alive?" I gasped.

"Yes, and told me the same thing you just did. But something doesn't seem quite right here. See," he leaned forward with his elbows on his knees, "it could all be chalked up to local gang activity, except the women floating in the lifeboats. Could be coincidence, but we've been tracking a group that has been travelling the world for a few years executing pimps and pedophiles and rescuing the victims, giving the credit for the rescues to various non-profits. This fits that MO. So, Dr. Burke, I'm going to come right out and ask: are you working for the

CIA? NSA? MI6?" His face was deadly serious.

Thanks to the medication, I found that part hilarious, so I giggled a little and shook my head. "No, no, of course not. I'm a professor."

He waited again, awkward silences being a part of good police work, I assume. "A woman named Rosa claimed responsibility for evacuating all the women. So, right now, it looks like you and Mr. Weiss are either the best secret agents the world has ever seen or the story he gave me is correct. That a woman, her boyfriend and his son all went for a ride and ended up in a very unlucky situation." He shrugged, looking back through his notes.

Ugh, boyfriend. Wait… "Did… did Ravi say he was my boyfriend?"

Detective Scott flipped through his notes and said, "Yes, he said the two of you have a relationship." He looked at me expectantly.

I blushed at this. "He's not my boyfriend. But I don't know, maybe he is. I mean, things have progressed with us, if that's what you're asking, but I don't know… who knows where this could go. But a relationship? Yeah, I would call it that," I stammered, beaming at the officer at this thought.

He rolled his eyes and shut his notebook, "Yeah, definitely not CIA," he started toward the door. "I'll call you if I have any more questions." And, just like that, we were off the hook. I sat shocked, trying to understand that my future wasn't gone. That I would see my children again. It was a sacrifice I had already accepted, so I could barely comprehend that I wouldn't spend my life in jail, or worse. I laid back down and cried until I fell asleep.

I was released the next morning with hospital issued scrubs and crutches along with a big bag of medications. I immediately hobbled to the nurse's station to ask where Ravi was. A nurse agreed to walk me to his room. My heart was racing, I didn't know what I was going to see. I opened the door carefully, he had a large tube coming out of his chest and multiple other tubes going all over his body and an oxygen tube under his nose. I sat in a chair next to his bed and grabbed his hand. He roused, looked over at me and sighed, "Mia".

"I'm here, its ok," I told him.

"I'm guessing you talked to the police as well?" he asked between breaths. Breathing seemed very difficult for him, I hated seeing that.

"Yes, he doesn't believe we're involved in the explosion at all. How did you do that?" I whispered.

Ravi gave a weak laugh. "I know you, Mia. I knew you would stick to the story. But the best part is I knew if I told him you were my girlfriend you would do one of two things: straight out deny it, which meant you didn't have feelings for me, or, you would blush and stammer like you always do when you're flustered, in which case we would be off the hook and I would know." It was really a genius plan.

"You would know what?"

"That you have feelings for me," he smiled impishly, even in his condition. I just blushed.

"Do you want to know what I said to you in Hebrew all those times we made love?" he asked.

"Yes," I was still blushing.

He sighed. "I told you all the things you weren't ready to hear but I desperately needed to tell you. I said I love you, I've loved you since the moment I met you, and you have my heart indefinitely." He looked directly into my eyes as he said this, and I knew he meant every word. He took a few deep breaths as my eyes welled with tears.

"I love you, too, Ravi." It felt so good to tell him and the tears fell down my cheeks.

In true Ravi fashion, he slowly raised his hand in the air and made a fist. "Yes! Finally, Mia!" I laughed through the tears. "You are the most stubborn woman in existence, it wasn't easy getting you to admit you love me, too," he laughed weakly. A nurse came in to check his vital signs and Ravi told her, "Hey, this beautiful woman over here loves me, and I love her. Isn't that incredible?" She smiled, not understanding a word he said and we both laughed about it. The nurse put an injection of something in his IV line and within moments he was asleep again. I grabbed his hand in both of mine, laid my head on his bed, and fell asleep next to him.

"Well, it's about time," I heard a familiar voice say.

I looked up toward the door and saw Eleora, her hair in loose waves around her shoulders. "You two should've realized how good you were together years ago," she laughed.

"What are you doing here?" I asked, still groggy.

"I was presenting at a medical conference in India and I heard what happened here. I tried to call Ravi, but when I didn't get an answer, I called Hassan. He told me you two were vacationing in the Philippines," she rolled her eyes. "Vacationing, indeed. So, I called all the hospitals until I found you two. How are you feeling?"

"Better," I said. I didn't tell her how worried I was about Ravi.

"Good. Because we need to talk." She pulled up a chair and as she did, the little boy walked around the hospital bed and grinned at me.

I gasped. "Eleora, what did you do?" I whispered angrily.

"What else could I do?" She leaned forward whispering. "When I went to see you the hospital staff were talking about placing him in state custody or an orphanage. I couldn't bear to see that sweet face go into one of those awful places, so I just walked in and told them he was my grandson. That his mother was killed in a terrible accident and Ravi was in the Philippines to pick him up and take custody." She looked at me guiltily.

She had gotten him some nice clothes, complete with new shoes and socks and he looked like a different child altogether. She had even gotten him a designer boys' haircut. He no longer looked like a refugee, but an active and happy child, except the gauze wrapped around his tiny hand to treat his burn. He was holding a bag of animal crackers and a juice box, and my heart swelled as he climbed gently into my lap and gave me a hug.

"How will you get him out of the country?" I asked.

"Ravi said he can make some very legitimate looking documents," she said with a guilty shrug. I believed her on that.

I sighed. It felt so wrong, but she was right. "Do you know what his name is?" I asked as the boy tried to share a gooey animal cracker with me.

"I've decided to call him Asher. It means 'fortunate' in Hebrew." She smiled when she said his name. *Fortunate, lucky.* I thought it ironic that a child from such horrible conditions who endured the nightmare of losing his mother the way he did should be considered lucky or fortunate. But, seeing his clean, happy, face as he tried to share his cracker with me, maybe he *is* lucky.

"There is something else we need to discuss," she turned serious. "Your flight is scheduled to leave tomorrow, correct?"

"Yes, I'll call and push it back. It shouldn't be a problem."

"It is a problem, Emelia. You are medically cleared to travel, and this isn't like Dubai. I think your children need you and you need to go home and see them."

"But I can't leave Ravi like this!" I gestured toward him, with all the tubes and wires. He still hadn't woken from his night's sleep.

"This is why I am here. I will personally supervise his care and ensure he makes it back home with Asher. I have a lot of pull in places like this," and she winked at me.

Leaving him in the care of his cardiovascular surgeon mother didn't seem all that risky, I just didn't want to. I wanted to see him wake up, hear his voice again, especially to hear him tell me he loves me. But Ethan was scheduled to tour some colleges next week, and I missed both of the kids. I didn't want to alarm them with another extended vacation and another horrible accident. I hated to admit she was right, and I felt my eyes sting with tears.

The nurse came in to check Ravi's vitals. Eleora continued, "I will go get you some clothes to travel home in, don't worry about that. I think you're making—" she was cut off by loud beeping from the machine the nurse was using. Eleora looked at the readings. "This can't be right, check it again." She grabbed the nurse's stethoscope roughly from her neck and began examining Ravi, listening to his breathing sounds. I waited nervously, fidgeting with my hair. Addressing the nurse, she said, "I need you to call your attending physician immediately and tell them the patient is developing an infection. It may be from poor insertion of the chest tube, but he needs a regimen of antibiotics beginning right now if we are going to prevent the need for more surgery." The nurse started to gather her supplies, when Eleora said, "I didn't say later, I said immediately. Go make the call right now." She had a way of speaking with terrifying authority without even raising her voice. The nurse jogged out of the room and Eleora rolled her eyes. She opened Ravi's chart and looked over it occasionally shaking her head in frustration.

"Will he be alright?" I asked. Now I really didn't want to leave.

"I will make sure he recovers from this; do you mind sitting with Asher while I go get you some clothes and have a discussion with the attending physician?"

"Of course I don't mind." And I didn't, I had missed his constant presence over the last few days and was happy to see how well he was doing. He jabbered at me in toddler speak, with me only able to really understand a few words of it like, "shoes" and "look". He walked all around the room showing me things, I forgot how curious toddlers were, it's been a while since my own children were this age, but I loved his curiosity and his rambunctious energy. It was a delight to see this boy who I only saw as a job become a thriving toddler.

Eleora returned with a bag for me and told me they would be moving Ravi to the intensive care unit and wouldn't be allowed visitors. I gasped, but she grabbed my hand and calmly told me it was for his own protection and she would take care of him. She gave me the key to her hotel room across the street and suggested I stay in her suite, since my flight left early in the morning. She picked up Asher and put him on her hip, giving me a reassuring hug. "I'll be in touch, dear." I kissed Ravi on the forehead and whispered *I love you* in his ear, gathered my things and walked out of the hospital, unsure if I would ever see Asher, Eleora, or Ravi again.

Of course, the suite was luxurious. I hobbled in on my crutches and decided to take a shower and really get a full look at the extent of my wounds. I went into the bathroom and it was almost like the moment in Ravi's flat, but I had long since let go of keeping myself completely put together, so it wasn't quite such a shock. My left cheek had a C-shaped slice that had dozens of fresh stitches. I sighed, it would leave an ugly scar, but I suppose it wasn't as though I had won any beauty contests before this. I expected the wound to my leg to look gruesome, since it had been infected and caused most of the complications during my hospital stay, but the wound was only six inches long and looked to be healing well. No drainage or separation between sutures. Aside from the crutches and the ugly slice on my face, maybe the kids wouldn't be too alarmed by my appearance. I showered carefully, dressed my wounds, then went to the big luxurious bed to get a good night's rest before facing everything at home. "Boating accident" sounded like a fine alibi, but I was tired. Tired of scaring the kids and Laura, tired of hurting, tired of everything.

20

Manchester—Boston Regional Airport New Hampshire

I hobbled down to the terminal on my crutches to meet Laura, who agreed to pick me up at the airport. When she saw me, she gasped and put her hands over her mouth. "Emelia, what… what happened?"

"I'll tell you in the car," I mumbled.

"Ok… I'll get your bags from baggage claim," she started to rush toward baggage claim.

"No, no. This is all I have," I said, gesturing toward my backpack.

She gave me a sympathetic look then hugged me hard. I couldn't contain it any longer and burst into tears. We stood like that in the terminal for a few moments, one woman embracing a broken woman. She led me to the car and helped me in.

"Do you want to talk about it?" she asked carefully on the ride to their house to get the kids.

"Not really. I will tell you, though, I've decided to stop with the "vacations". We got in over our heads this time and I can't keep doing this," I wiped some stray tears away.

She reached over and grabbed my hand. We drove the rest of the way in silence, and I was grateful. She pulled over before we reached the house. "Are you ready for this? I want to make sure you can keep it together for the kids. If we need to go get a coffee or whatever to give you more time, we can." I took a deep breath and nodded. She drove down the long driveway and Jenna and

Ethan bounced out the door. When I got out of the car, they both stopped, gasping.

"It was just a boating accident, I'm ok." They both ran to me, hugging me, Jenna in tears and Ethan telling me it was ok. I looked at both of their faces and told them, "I think that will be my last vacation, my luck may not hold up for another one," and faked a laugh but it worked. They laughed, too, and hugged me some more.

January 2020

New Hampshire

It took a while to recover from everything that happened. I spent a week at home with Jenna and Ethan, they fussed over me and brought me drinks and snacks while Max purred contentedly on my lap as we binge watched Netflix. By then, I couldn't delay talking to the people at work about it, so I decided asking for a leave of absence would be most appropriately done in person. Ethan drove me to the Dean's office and by then I was limping still and using a cane. I walked into his office, expecting the worst.

"Dr. Burke, oh my Lord what happened?" was the first response I got from him. He had been doing some work on his computer and did a double take when I walked into his office.

"Boating accident on vacation. That's actually why I'm here, I need to take a leave of absence." I knew the fresh scar on my face would have a startling effect and hoped it might invoke a little sympathy instead of anger. It worked.

"No problem, we'll hire some adjunct staff and cover your classes until...?"

"Fall?" I thought I might be ready by then, but with the kind of work I do, there was really no telling.

"Fall it is. I certainly hope you have a speedy recovery, we'll all be thinking of you," he said with genuine concern.

I thanked him and walked back to the car slowly. I had been dreading that all week and felt a huge sense of relief. It turns out his concern was sincere; a huge bouquet of flowers arrived at the house a few days later with a card signed by the entire department staff. He made the subtle offer to work from home or do research as I recover, but I didn't want to. I didn't want to read, research, or even think about human trafficking for a while.

Not to mention, I had three physical therapy appointments twice a week and they were intense and grueling. I was assigned a young man named Monty who seemed very gentle and soft-spoken, until he's pushing you through the most intense pain. "You're a runner, Emelia, and I plan on making you a runner again at the end of this!" I powered through these sessions almost as though they were psychotherapy, letting myself enjoy the pain, pushing myself as hard as I could. Though it felt like torture, it was helping in more ways than just physically.

I did find myself, though, struggling to know what to do with myself at first. I cleaned the house entirely too much, started a vegetable garden, began cooking foreign food (the kids didn't much care for those experiments), read a few novels I had always meant to read, took a yoga class recommended by Monty but still at the end of the day, something was always missing, and I felt lonely and alone. I cried a lot, and for no reason, and often just wandered around the house aimlessly. I was doing all the right things to cope with everything and to move forward with life, but it felt empty somehow.

Ethan and I toured a few colleges close by, but ultimately, he decided on Boston College, pre-med. "You really want to be a doctor?" I asked excitedly on the way home.

"Yeah, I didn't take all those AP science classes for no

reason," he grinned at me.

I didn't want to embarrass him by gushing about how terribly proud I was of him, so I just grabbed his hand, squeezed, and said, "You're a good man, Ethan."

He blushed anyway and gave me the standard, "Aw, thanks, mom." Every time he blushed, he reminded me of when he was a little boy, my heart ached at that memory.

May 2020

Now, it's late spring, which is a lovely time of year in New Hampshire. I moved my seedlings outside and now have a fully-fledged garden of sprouts that I care for as if they were little children. Ethan is about to graduate, Jenna is sailing effortlessly through her classes, still giving me teenage girl drama about social media (which I banned), curfew, and basically everything. She's a fierce girl and I hope she stays fierce forever. She runs with me now every day, a slow steady pace for just two or three miles. I'm hoping to build up my strength for longer runs in the fall, maybe even a marathon. But for now, I just enjoy the time alone with her.

And that's how it all happened. That's how I became a serial killer and that's how I stopped. I still don't feel guilty about it, but certain aspects of the missions still haunt me. I think about Rosa, I think about her a lot and wonder how she made out after that mess. I think of the children in Dubai, the woman in Haiti and her baby that she wanted to keep safe. That's the hardest part of everything we did, Ravi always tried to reassure me that we were making a difference, but I just had to take that on faith and hope that luck went with them after their liberation. He always believed so much in what we were doing, it was his passion and I like to think that if nothing else, it gave him purpose and fulfillment. He deserved that from the world and from me.

192

Now, I'm drinking coffee on the deck, admiring the sprouts in the garden and thinking about how much life had changed since January. I stretched the soreness out of my right leg and opened up the paper, flipping through to my favorite parts. I was just about to go inside for a refill, when the door opened and a tall man with a beautiful mop of black hair brought out a fresh cup and my whole wheat toast that he knows I love. Ravi sat next to me, caressing the fading scar on my cheek and sipped his coffee. "Are you almost done with the paper? We only have a few more minutes and I'd like to get a look," he asked me casually. I handed him the paper and took a bite of toast. He was right, we only had minutes left of this glorious peace. He reached over and grabbed my left hand, running his thumb over the diamond on the third finger as he read over the front page. We sat in silence, enjoying the sounds of the morning, the birds, the squirrels chittering in the trees. The silence was suddenly shattered by the door slamming and the thumping of little feet running across the deck.

"Daddy! Mummy!" Asher squealed, still in his Paw Patrol footie pajamas and he dove into our laps. He had wild bed hair and a big sleepy grin. "Cereal?" he asked. Then he put his hands on his cheeks and cocked his head to the side, "Peeeez?" We laughed and couldn't resist.

Ravi threw him over his shoulder while Asher squealed delightedly, "Guess that didn't last long," he said as he gave me a wink that went straight to my heart, just as it always had.

21
Two years later
Hanover, New Hampshire

Asher and TJ stood side by side on stage, fidgeting with their little diplomas while the whole family cheered and took pictures. They were graduating pre-k and the prestigious pre-k put on a big show for the families that doled out such ridiculous amounts in tuition. They even gave them tiny caps and gowns, we all loved it. Eleora had taken a position in Boston to be closer and never missed a family event, I think she even had tears in her eyes as they called Asher's name. When the ceremony was over, Laura and I posed the boys in front of an extravagant backdrop to get about a hundred pictures while Bryce and Ravi rolled their eyes. We joked that we'll be using those pictures at their high school graduation, we had no doubt they would stay close, they called each other brother and were practically inseparable.

We were meeting Ethan for a celebration lunch nearby, but I think he just wanted to go to see Eleora. He read all her articles and they would talk for hours about her work; he loved to pick her brain and was certain he wanted to be a cardiothoracic surgeon after hearing all her stories. She loved all the adoration and promised to write her grandson a glowing recommendation letter for medical school when he needed it. Ravi just laughed; he knew Ethan didn't need it since he was acing all his classes, but he knew that she would provide it anyway.

I had nothing but admiration for Eleora since she was the biggest factor in Ravi coming to the US. She supervised his care in the hospital in Manilla, just as she promised, even standing in on the surgery to remove a portion of his infected lung. In all, he spent a month in the hospital, and she took complete charge of his care, ordering the staff around, all while taking care of Asher. Just before he was discharged, she gave Ravi a laptop, which apparently was all he needed to create a very official looking birth certificate for Asher. After that, getting him out of the Philippines was no problem, just a father taking his son home. Eleora stayed with Ravi in his flat helping him care for Asher while he recovered. A few weeks in, however, she started to notice the exact same symptoms I had during my recovery. That Ravi seemed empty and listless. She sat next to him one day and simply blurted it out, "You know, Dartmouth is looking for computer science professors. One, of your caliber, would bring a lot of prestige to the department." She said this casually, almost off-hand. Ravi sat for a moment, then immediately started packing suitcases for him and Asher.

He showed up on my doorstep a week later, dressed in a suit and tie (which I remember thinking was oddly formal for him) and I didn't even comprehend that Ravi, my Ravi, was standing on my doorstep until he spoke.

"Emelia." He took a step forward, smiling.

"Oh, Ravi," I wrapped my arms around him and tried to soak up every detail about him in that moment, his smell, the texture of his hands, the warmth coming from his chest. Then, Asher dashed in the door squeezing between us and I scooped him up and we all held each other, and I finally felt like I had come home.

We never discussed him staying, he was just there, and it was right and that was all that mattered. About a week later he told me over breakfast that Dartmouth called him, and he got the job. I squealed and jumped into his lap kissing him excitedly, which

195

made Asher laugh and Jenna say, "Come on, get a room!" with a laugh. That sort of made it all official, the next day we decided to make the upstairs guest bedroom Asher's room and painted it sky blue, his favorite color. Ravi surprised me by bringing in a twin bed, but it was shaped like a pirate ship.

I watched Asher jump on it saying, "I'm a piwate!" and looked at Ravi with my eyebrows raised and he couldn't hold his laughter in any longer, he doubled over laughing, telling me "I mean, he's kind of a pirate, too."

Ravi was an endlessly patient and thorough parent. He took great care teaching Asher things that he hadn't learned in his previous upbringing. We thought he was potty trained, but it turned out he would just drop his pants and "go" wherever he was. Ravi and I cleaned up plenty of messes those first few weeks, and Ravi would sit on the floor in front of Asher on his little potty and sing him songs in Hebrew while both of them clapped their hands. It always baffled me, seeing this man who could coolly put a pistol to a pedophile's head and execute him without flinching now singing "ABCs" and cutting hot dogs in tiny pieces so Asher wouldn't choke.

He wasn't just a good parent to Asher, either. When Jenna talked to him about her day he *actually* listened, interested in who her friends were and how her classes were going. He taught her shortcuts for her advanced math classes and told her how those classes are important in his work, how they have real world relevance. They also played fiercely competitive chess games in which one or the other would inevitably get frustrated and accuse the other of cheating. They made me laugh with that, those two trying to outsmart each other.

And that's just how life was for us. Shortly after he arrived came the ring, flashy enough for Ravi's taste, subtle enough for mine. Then in summer, a small Jewish ceremony in the backyard with just us and the kids with a rabbi attending. I traded jujitsu for yoga, which Ravi attended with me and we had weekly dates at the range, which were vastly different than my range date with Jonathan. We both enjoyed our work, loved our family, and he still said beautiful Hebrew things to me while we made love.

One night in bed he was holding me and on the verge of sleep when I asked him, "What took you so long to come here after the Philippines?"

He thought about that for a moment. "Honestly, I didn't know that I was supposed to. I thought you were here, and I was there, and that was that. It didn't even occur to me until mother mentioned it. I've never really been in this kind of situation before."

"What situation?" I asked.

"Oh, Mia, you know... women, dating, whatever." He kind of blushed.

"Ravi Weiss, are you saying you've only been in one relationship your whole life?" I was teasing him, like he teased me in Mexico, but it was honestly a surprise. He was very good at it.

He rolled his eyes at me. "Yes, Emelia, you are my first. My one and only. Forever." He jumped up and flexed his muscles, "Only one woman could tame this stallion!" We laughed and laughed at that.

"Really, Ravi? Only one?" He pinned me down and reminded me why I was his one and only.

One evening, Ravi and I were working in our shared office that we had remodeled the week before, with Jenna's help moving things in and out as necessary, when Jenna came to the door. "I need to talk to you," she said. Ravi looked at me and started to get up, but she said, "Both of you." This felt oddly like the conversation I had with Ethan all those years ago, but we stopped and gave her our full attention.

"When we were moving things last week, I saw some things in your files, Mom, that I don't think I was supposed to see. It was pictures and reports from an island in the Philippines, and it was all about sex trafficking. I know you weren't working on that at the time, but it was from right before your vacation and your 'accident'," she had actually made air quotes with her fingers. This couldn't be good. I glanced at Ravi, he had his brow furrowed and crossed his arms.

"I did a little research. I found some things about a yacht explosion, a bunch of women rescued. So, I looked into it some more and started to connect the dots. Your accident in Dubai that coincided with a huge rescue of children, your time in Punta Cana and a rescue in Haiti, I started to see a pattern. And, I noticed certain gang members mysteriously found dead at the same time. It took some work, but I found all this online. I have to ask, and you have to promise to be honest... was it you two?"

Ravi looked down then looked at me. I sighed. She was only seventeen.

"Yes." I tucked my hair behind my ear and waited for her response.

She nodded, thinking about it for a few moments. "You know you went about it all wrong. Taking trips to foreign locations and shooting people? Seriously? Let me show you something." She went to my computer and opened up a Facebook account with her name on it.

"Jenna, we talked about this—"

"Yes, and you were right. I opened this last year and within two days *this* is what happened." She opened up messenger and showed me all the men who were saying lewd things to her, propositioning her, and even sending explicit pictures.

Ravi jumped up, his jaw clenched, "You know I can find out where these men live in a matter of seconds." His fists were clenched as well.

"I know," Jenna said, "that's the point. Sexual predators are so easy to find online. Some of them may be harmless but some of them are probably doing this to lots of girls and even meeting them in person. I deactivated this account within two days, but I still have the evidence... and an idea."

"Jenna," Ravi said, "you're only seventeen and these men can be dangerous."

"Which means I'm still a minor and those men," she said, pointing to the computer screen, "they committed felonies by sending me that garbage. I'm not saying they all need to be shot, just saying we find out who really needs to be taught a lesson and have them come to us. Meet in a park or something, cuff them to a park bench with screenshots of the conversations and call the police. We have to do something."

"Um, *we*?" I asked.

"Yes." She stood a little taller. "I want in."

Ravi and I looked at each other, totally bewildered. She had not only found out about our secret, but critiqued it and thought up her own plan. And she wants in? "She's so your daughter," Ravi said with a laugh.

I should've tried to tame that wild spirit after all, I thought shaking my head and laughing.

Made in the USA
Middletown, DE
24 July 2021